7/18/21

The Spells of Lamazee

The Spells of Lamazee

An Historical Novel of the Pacific Northwest Coast

by James Seeley White

A DIVISION OF *Breitenbush Publications*

Library of Congress Card #82-14578
ISBN 0-932576-12-5
First printing

LOKI BOOKS is a division of Breitenbush Publications, Portland, Oregon. Mailing address: P.O. Box 02137, Portland, Oregon 97202.

The cover art is from a pen and pencil drawing by Laurie Levich.

Introduction

As the decades have passed, the memory of Lamazee's presence at Nehalem has faded. Early fears of the savage Killamuks continued, and it was not until 1840 that the first missionary, Joseph H. Frost, ventured through the land of Nehalem; nearly thirty more years passed before white settlers populated the valley.

The Indians, now known as the Tillamooks, are a people whose faint pathways, overgrown house pits, and shell mounds are studied by archaeologists. The mossy giants of the rain forest have been felled by the lumbermen's saws. Paved highways carry motorists swiftly over routes where Nehalem and fur trader toiled, missing the glimpses of wildlife, the taste of wild berries, and the thrill of adventure.

Sand dunes have moved in to cover the village along the shores of picturesque Nehalem Bay, dunes that may hide the lodge pits and fire rings forever, for they are held there by the roots of scrub pines and grasses. Across the bay, where the dark ship lies, only the ballast rock remains, hidden at times by shifting river channels, revealed at other times to curious divers.

The remains of the *TONQUIN* have never been discovered despite expeditions to find it. However, the expeditions have focused on Clayoquot Sound—where Lamazee told Captain Sheffield it had been destroyed.

Many people have searched for the wealth that the Nehalem legends say was buried, treasure that is popularly known as "the Treasure of Neahkanie Mountain." Some say that marked rocks point to where it lies buried; others say that the rocks are survey markers. Many have looked, and two have lost their lives in the quest.

A seaport community, Astoria, occupies the area where tiny, log-constructed Fort George served as the isolated outpost of the fur traders of the North West Fur Company. The peaceful hum of the town has replaced the quiet tension that held the Fort in 1814. Then, the loss of two ships, several traders to hostile up-river Indians, and the threats of the War of 1812 had caused the Fort to be sold. Indians with furs to trade were arriving less often and their visits were brief.

One

"To arms! Savages! To arms!" came the piercing cry from the log tower in the corner of the fort closest to the timber.

Men clad in buckskins and woolen garments against the crispness of an autumn morning came tumbling out of roughhewn buildings at opposite sides of the stockade. Clutching powder horns and rifles, they scrambled into the two corner towers situated at opposite extremes of Fort George. The men readied themselves to place a sweeping fire before the rows of vertical, sharp-pointed logs of the stockade wall.

Leading the rush to the fortifications was a stocky, auburn-haired Scotsman, rifle and powder flask caught up in one hand, a brass telescope in the other. He dropped his gaze from the stockade momentarily as he passed the bare earth of a grave and scowled, seemingly scanning the carved letters in the wooden marker. "A.E. Judge, murdered by Killamuks, 1814."

Then he hastened up the wooden stairs. Squinting through a rifle slit, the Scotsman could see nothing moving in the open ground between the fort and the hillside. Tree stumps in the cleared ground might hide enemies—it was unfortunate they had not been able to finish the task of burning them out. Little mounds of earth covered the Indians they had captured and executed, but they were not large enough to conceal a man. Nothing moved. "Where are they, Mr. Frazer, where?"

"Over there, sir, running through the timber. I have barely been able to make them out at times, but it appears to be a long file circling the fort."

Duncan McDougal's square Scottish face was even ruddier than usual as he extended the telescope for a clearer view. He was still puffing from his rapid climb up the ladder and having difficulty steadying the glass.

"Hmm-m." Duncan had the telescope extended and focused and was trying to sweep the edge of the forest with his gaze.

"There they are, sir, more to your left now and up the hillside. You can catch an occasional glimpse of them between the trees—a long line of heathens coming in around us."

"Hmm-m." McDougal continued, resting the instrument on the log sill. This steadied it, and he was beginning to make out something brown and moving. "Oh, yes—."

The image was disrupted as he flinched from the roar of a rifle at his side and a cry of "There they come!" Several other weapons added their thunder, and puffs of smoke obscured McDougal's vision.

Firing stopped as abruptly as it began. In the silence the flails of death throes could be heard at the edge of the clearing, while outside of the bastion, a man's muted laughter could be heard. McDougal flushed, "Mister Frazer, those are elk. What you have been seeing is a herd running through the forest. They were probably frightened by a catamount."

The young man turned and stammered, "I'm terribly sorry, sir." Other youths at the rifle slits looked embarrassed, too, but continued to stare out over the clearing to where a brown animal the size of a large cow lay on its side. It was quiet now, with its massive, dark head still up, looking blankly along the edge of the timber it had unfortunately left. Then it slowly lowered its head and was silent.

McDougal paused, blustery and irritated, holding his tongue for the moment. "Very well, stay alert." The response showed unusual restraint for him.

Duncan McDougal was naturally ill-tembered, but he was sufficiently perceptive not to add to the tensions of the post by strongly upbraiding the lookout. The man would take enough jibes from the other young men when he returned from duty. Besides, Frazer did not have the benefit of the telescope that McDougal jealously guarded.

The other two young men who had fired at the elk scurried down the ladder ahead of Duncan McDougal. They were stopped as they reached the ground, and now were being addressed by a man with an even stronger Scottish accent.

"Ver-ry well, laddies, we do nae want that meat to spoil. Ye both take skinning knives and pack boards wi'ye and go fetch in the hide and meat from yon cow.

"Do nae worry. Mister Frazer will keep a fine watch that no heathens get ye. But mind ye, hurry along." He could see their hesitation, and his soft-spoken words were reassuring.

"Yes, sir, Mister McTavish." The two clerks knew they could have been reprimanded for firing without orders, and they knew that going out to the far side of the clearing to perform a chore of that magnitude was, in a way, punishment. They did not argue, for they perceived the soft-spoken words as being still firm and authoritative. As the Scotsman watched, the two quickly gathered their assigned equipment, reloaded their rifles, and hastened through the gate. The officer stepped over and replaced the heavy wooden beam that barred a gate so small a man had to step high and duck low to pass through.

McDougal was red-faced and swearing as he climbed down the ladder and entered the building where his companions had preceded him. Men looked up from where they were cleaning, reloading, and placing weapons back on pegs in the log walls. "M'Tavish," Duncan sputtered, addressing the tall Scotsman standing beside the stone fireplace, "we must do something about this damnable mess."

"Aye, the two clerks have already been sent to fetch the meat and hide from the elk. The workout from the protection of the fort should be sufficient to keep them from firing before ordered again."

"No, that is not what I mean. We are obliged to make an expedition to find out what the problem is. If the Indians won't come to us to trade, we must go to their villages. We have to get their furs for the Fort to be profitable. They are the only peltries that don't cost us a lot of supplies and men to go after. If we become dependent on bringing furs all the way from the Snake and upper Columbia Rivers, we will have to close Fort George.

"Since the Indians have stopped bringing the local furs to us, we must go to the Indians and get the trade going again."

The tall Scotsman did not respond immediately but stood pondering the suggestion. John George McTavish was known for his tactful forcefulness, and the wee-thought-out decisions in his new role of Principal Agent. He was obviously thinking over McDougal's pronouncement, for he had creased his heavy dark eyebrows and placed a hand to his thin beard. "Aye, that is bad. But the problems with the men are my immediate concern. We must do somethin' to ease their minds.

"But, I do nae like your thought. Are ye forgetting what happened to Jacob Rezner, Pierre Dorion, Giles LeClerc, John Reed, and all the others at the hands of those murderous Nez Perce a scant three years ago? And poor Judge's broken bones are hardly settled in his grave.

"I ken the situation. We need the furs that are brought to us to offset the cost of those we must travel to buy, and wi'out them the Fort may fail. Perhaps we should go to the Indian villages and encourage them to trade, but we might also lose our lives and gain nae a thing.

"The signs are bad, mon. Look before the fort—toward the river. The women have left their hootches and gone back to their tribes. Somethin' must be aboot."

McDougal shook his stocky head so clumps of dark auburn hair swirled about; he spat into the fire and sputtered, "They have gone only because there are no men to buy their filthy services. The spring gathering is over, no ships have been in, and these lads are too fearful for their sap to be a-running. They don't venture outside the stockade walls any longer than their chores demand, certainly not long enough to crawl into one of those hutches and roll around with a squaw."

As McDougal paused to utter an oath, McTavish pondered how the stocky man had lost both his Scottish accent and manners during his employment with the Americans.

"We haven't been troubled by the Clatsops in the past, and the Killamuks would have attacked by now if they were bent on it. I know we haven't dealt with the Killamuks a lot, but the band that lives closest, the Nehalem group, should have been here to trade these last months. Earlier they traded with us regularly. If we don't find out what the Killamuks are up to, we are going to be jumping to arms every time a herd of elk or some lone deer moves along the trees. Besides, our garden is going to weeds, and if this wariness continues we won't get our winter victuals put up.

"I think we should travel to the Nehalem place and find out. If that redheaded fellow that lives with them, Lamazee, would come around we could question him, but we haven't seen him since the *TONQUIN* was lost. We must go to him."

"Ooh, ye're assumin they have nae split his skull."

McDougal shook his head emphatically again, and turned from the fire to face the taller, more slender companion. "He gets along fine with them. It's us he doesn't take to, M'Tavish."

"Aye, and I do nae know that I would trust what he said anyway. There is something strange about that one. Did ye ever notice the way he looks at ye? He watches ye carefully, but his eyes always turn away when ye look back at him. I would nae trust him not to be the first to put the knife to my throat."

"At least he has taught the Indians enough that we can communicate with them.

"What would you say to an inland trek? We could cross the mountain and follow a stream down to the Nehalem village. It would be less exposed than going by sea."

McTavish stood silently, considering the idea for several minutes before responding, "I do nae know—I do nae feel well aboot it. For one thing, we do nae know aboot the loyalties of the Clatsop villages we would pass along the plain, and I have the feeling that the band at the southern end of the plain, the Nehaynehum, may actually be Killamuk instead of Clatsop. It is only the Killamuk people that call their villages by words starting with 'Ne'—like Ne-halem and Ne-stocka. The Clatsops and Chinooks don't use those sounds."

"I don't see how you could hope to tell them apart." From across the room came the voice of Doctor Swan, the post surgeon, who had been sitting on a rough bench, listening to the conversation and adding puffs of smoke from his pipe to the haziness lent to the room by the ill-drawing fireplace. "They all look alike with their flattened, deformed craniums, and eyes popped out like those of a mouse in a trap." Dr. Swan shook his head in disbelief at this phenomenon so incompatible with his study of craniology or phrenology.

McTavish spoke again. "We should seek council from M'Kenzie; he is in command of the post. If only there were some way to get word to him, but a messenger might nae even be able to find the trade expedition in the vastness of the Columbia basin—even if he did get past the villainous band at Wishram.

"Perhaps we could persuade some of the Chinooks to transport us to the Nehalem village in their canoes. It would be faster, and wouldn't leave the garrison weakened for so long. Aye, that could be a lot easier."

"I know, M'Tavish," came the sarcastic reply, "it would be a lot more comfortable, but we would be quite exposed sitting in canoes. Besides, during this time of year we can only travel by canoe in the mornings. We would have to land on the beach each day as the afternoon gales come up. There we would be ready targets for Killamuk arrows."

The sarcasm faded as McDougal sought to sell his point. "I didn't mean to weaken the post by taking a force out. You and I could make it by land. We could slip away while the rest stayed on guard; the Indians won't even notice if we lay our plans right.

"Besides, all of the tribes are canoeing peoples. They spend so much time on the water they have become short-legged and stocky, much better at sitting in a canoe paddling than running through the forest. I would consider our chances much better inland if we have to run for our lives."

"Ye make it sound very reasonable, Duncan, but it would be a very difficult trip through the Devil's Club, nettles, and brush." McTavish obviously didn't like the prospects, for he sat down upon the hearth, and looked with furrowed brow at the hard-packed dirt floor for a long, silent time. After a while he readied his eyes and gazed out the doorway to the sun's rays slanting through the sharpened tips of the vertical logs of the stockade walls.

McDougal waited, giving the thoughtful McTavish an opportunity to consider the options. It was difficult, for McDougal was inclined to act impulsively, but he had learned that his superior must make up his own mind, and that argument would only bring out stubborn resistance.

"What were ye thinking, M'Dougal, of crossing the peninsula and taking a bearing up Young's River to the mountains?"

"No, that would take too long."

"What then? If we follow the coastal plain we will be seen and just as vulnerable to any michief of the Clatsops as we would be in a canoe. I do nae think we could possibly make it through the swamp along the edge of the narrow plain, and the mosquitoes are terrible. We would probably catch swamp fever and succumb. And, do ye nae think we should take a force with us?"

"Look what we have. Frazer, Stuart, the M'Tavish brothers, and the other clerks haven't been here long enough to finish their apprenticeships. They are idiots that would lose their way in the forest. M'Gillivray might do well, but he is needed to keep the fort in order while we are gone. M'Kenzie and George Keith took all our engagés on their trading expeditions. Even that writer, Cox, has gone wandering off on one of his visits, so that leaves us." McDougal lowered his voice, and stepping closer to the agent, continued, "I was thinking of shortening the time by going down the beach. If we traveled at night and kept up a brisk pace we could be at the far end of the plain and into the cover of the timber on the first headland by dawn. The Clatsops don't move about much during the night, and the waves of the high tide would wash away our footprints."

"Where then?"

"We would use the deer and elk trails along the stream that flows to the sea this side of the headland, and follow it into the mountains. When we have proceded sufficiently, we will have gone around the mountains the Indians call Neahkanie, passing to the east. In due time we should discover a stream that flows southward, and by following it would be led to the bay where the Nehalem lodges are. We can take the telescope with us, that we may watch from a distance to see what they are up to. If it appears to be war, we will return to Fort George unannounced."

John McTavish rose from the hearth and selected a beeswax candle from the mantle. Raising a burning stick from the fire momentarily, he lit the candle and carried it to the table. The light from the doorway and rifle ports was not sufficient for him to study the rude map that he unrolled.

In silence, the men gathered around the table: McTavish, McDougal, and Doctor Swan. The chart was well detailed along the coast, in those portions within sight of a sailing ship, and through the land they had traveled with the friendly Chinooks and Clatsops. Beyond those portions, however, in the area where Duncan McDougal proposed to travel, the paper was blank.

"Well," McTavish spoke at last, "it is probably as sound a plan as we hae available. I make it to be aboot ten leagues of beach from the Columbia to the mountainous headland. Can we cover that much during darkness?"

"We must, M'Tavish. By marching at a brisk pace we should be able to gain a league-and-a-half each hour. We will make the distance easily in six or seven hours, for there are no large streams or other obstructions along the route. Dawn should find us well hidden in the forest."

"Ver-ry well, but let's carry out our duties of the day, then sleep on it. We can do some more planning tomorrow morning."

"Fine." The decision had been made, and McDougal seemed satisfied.

Through the day, work details were carried out with a flourish. Drying furs were checked and turned, gardens were tended, firewood was brought in and stacked, and chinking that had fallen from between the logs of the buildings as the wood shrank during the dryness of summer was replaced.

The following day was one of planning and preparation for the journey. McTavish and McDougal would take little with them, so they might move quickly, and everything carried must be of vital importance. Because they would not intend to stand and fight, they carried a limited powder supply. Provisions consisted primarily of dried venison, to be supplemented by berries along the trail, for they had no wish of risking either the sound of a shot to provide fresh meat nor the sight of a fire for cooking. They would not even be able to utilize the potato-like wappitoo roots, for they needed to be roasted or boiled to diminish their bitter taste.

Clothing suited for damp weather was arranged and mended as clouds normally lurked about the peaks of Neahkanie, and there was no way of knowing how far into the mists the travelers might be compelled to venture in search of a route.

Preparations were also made for those remaining at the fort. Daily routines must appear normal, but no trading was to take place. If the Indians were denied entrance to the post there would be less liklihood of McDougal's and McTavish's absence being discovered. Besides, the fort would be further weakened by two rifles, and more prone to become the victim of treachery without the experienced leaders. None of the tribes-people were to be allowed inside; if they asked to enter they were to be told there was sickness.

By afternoon the two had laid out their provision, shot, and powder, and placed the affairs of the post in order. They ate a hearty meal, their last for many days to come.

Both men sought to gain some rest during the day, for they knew the night would be taxing. However, the anticipation of the voyage kept both awake and restless. Despite knowing they could not rest again until they were a safe distance from the coastline, they had felt compelled to spend most of the day in activity.

As evening approached, it was time to put their plan into operation. The wind was diminishing and shadows lengthened. The night would be calm, but faint puffs of ocean-spawned fog were drifting onto the land. The moon would be hidden, its light dimmed by clouds.

Before the post, several men appeared making ready for an evening hunting party. They all carried light packs, the type normally carried to contain the materials for cutting up a venison secured for the table. They seemed to be conversing jovially as they drew a canoe to the shore and climbed into it. However, the talk was not of hunting.

"Well, M'Tavish," asked his stocky companion, "are you satisfied with the plan?"

"Aye, posing as a hunting party will give us an early start on our trek down the beach. I do hope any Clatsops that might be watching cannae count the men in the canoe, but I feel more comfortable than trying to make the entire distance to the headland in darkness."

"Hmmph," McDougal snorted. "What else do your feelings tell you about our journey?"

McTavish tried to force a smile, but made no reply. It was Doctor Swan that responded. "Don't be so skeptical, Duncan. It has been scientifically established in phrenology that individuals with cranial configurations like John's have great intuitive powers. Some are able to communicate soundlessly, and over great distances, with others."

"Poppycock!" McDougal interrupted. "All I need is to have some sort of mystic along on a trip like this." He turned as though to stop paddling.

"Hold on, McDougal, I didn't mean there is anything unnatural about John. He simply has a cranial development conducive to great perceptiveness."

"Perhaps, but I shall rely on my telescope to give me my perceptions. I've heard of your 'abilities,' M'Tavish, but we have to be dead certain of what we see, else we will simply be dead."

Finally, the taller, dark-haired McTavish brought an end to the tone of conversation. "Don't ye carry a care in that realm, M'Dougal. I'm in no way governed by visions; I'm nae a mystic."

Past the tip of the wooded peninsula the canoers paddled, moving down the wide estuary with the outgoing tide. Gliding across the calm, glittering waters at the mouth of Young's River, they headed toward the bushy sand dunes along the south shore of the Columbia. Still out away from the bank, beyond the range of arrows, they passed a small party of Clatsops. On they moved, until they reached a small river that flowed into the wide Columbia. Here they turned, making no measure of concealment, for this was to be a peaceful hunting group.

For a time they canoed south along the small stream, then, as it made an abrupt turn, they beached the canoe on the west bank and assumed a hunting posture. Spreading out, they hiked westward, working steadily through the brush and trees in the direction of the Pacific surf. No Indians appeared, but they generally avoided the path of hunting parties. Perhaps it was the code of gentlemen of the forest not to interfere with another's hunt; perhaps it was their concern of a stray rifle ball.

Light faded, and the hazy western sky turned from pink to crimson. The hunting party had split. Some of the hunters returned to the canoe and made ready to return to the fort. Two, though, had wandered off to the south and sat between the dunes, watching the fiery red disc settle into the sea, signifying the end of another day. Seemingly they had not yet found their game, and were intent upon sleeping out that night, to catch the unwary deer feeding at first light.

It was fast becoming dark as the canoe passed the Clatsops on the shore. The craft was far out into the river on its return, as it had been earlier when heading out for the hunt; the paddlers, packs, and a few bits of driftwood for the fire were obscure in the dusk. Darkness would fall before the gates of the fort opened and closed for them.

"Well, M'Dougal, shall we start?"

"Yes, but let's wander north until we reach the wave line, then double south where the surf will sweep away our tracks."

"Ver-ry well. I am anxious to cover as much distance as I can, though, before the mist thickens."

"Don't fret about the fog. It will help to conceal us."

"Aye, but it will also hide any Clatsops or Killamuks."

The two men strolled leisurely toward the beach, angling their path northerly, toward the shoals at the mouth of the Columbia. The roar and hiss of the surf seemed louder from that direction as the waves stormed over miles of shallow sandbars. When they had gone a short distance, they stopped at the edge of the wave's sweep, then strolled just as leisurely to the south. They moved onward. Then, as if by signal, McDougal took the lead and their pace quickened. Within a quarter of a mile they were concealed by the night.

In silence they marched along, always on the wet sand that would be swept by the next wave, occasionally with the foamy edge of the wave lapping about their clothing as the sea mist increased. The cold, clammy air had enclosed them. They could neither see beyond the churning of the closest breakers nor past the dark gray sillhouettes of the dunes. After an hour or more had passed McDougal paused at the edge of a small stream whose waters spread wide and shallow where it mingled with the surf.

"So far," he said, as McTavish drew up and squatted beside him, "everything seems quiet. If we have passed any lodges, the Clatsops have settled in, out of the wetting. With this fog it would be difficult to know us if someone did see us."

"Ooh, they would know we were from the fort, all right. Neither of us are short of leg like the natives. Nor do we smell of fish oil—the mists cannae hide that."

"Don't have a care, M'Tavish. They are all holed up in the huts with their squaws."

"Shall I take the lead for a while?"

"Fine."

The pace resumed, the adventurers moving briskly along the beach. They were still careful to stay close to the edge of the waves, but they needn't endure the cold water at their ankles any more, for the tide was out, and would cover their tracks as it returned before morning. The moon had risen and was full above the mist, its round whiteness reflected in pools of seepage on the wet sand. A space filled with an eerie light seemed to exist between the men and the white curtain of fog. It was not unlike being in the broad spotlight of a stage, being illuminated before shadowed faces the actors could not discern.

Abruptly, McTavish stopped, raising his rifle more sharply in the cradle of his left arm. He stood for a moment, then cautiously squatted, peering into the darkness before him. McDougal walked slowly up beside him, rifle poised, and looked carefully around. Two dark shapes reposed on the beach before them, nearly prone figures with heads raised. The figures were immobile, and directly in the path.

"What do you make of them? Are they Clatsops?" McDougal asked softly.

"I do nae know. Probably driftwood logs—though I thought one moved, and 'tis nae usual for drift to be out on the sand instead of at the high tide line."

"Have you made out anything near the dunes?"

"No, nae yet, but let's hold and watch."

For the next ten minutes or so, time that seemed like hours, the two men crouched, rifles at ready. McTavish shifted his weight as a cramp struck his leg, but neither spoke. Finally, the cramp overcoming his concerns, McTavish stood erect. He turned his attentions toward the land, carefully scrutinizing the dunes, then quietly spoke. "Let's be on; they are merely logs."

"Hold a bit more, M'Tavish. The one on the left appears to have moved. Don't they seem closer together?"

Again silence reigned, though McTavish remained upright. After another five minutes of intense watching, McDougal also stood up.

"All right, it must have been my eyes. Let's move on, but cautiously. It could be an ambush."

Slowly they cocked their rifles, then with the weapons at ready, they moved forward. The two separated slightly, to be less of a target for arrows. Distances closed; the objects remained immobile and seemed less human in shape.

McTavish lowered the hammer of his rifle and quickened his pace to draw alongside his companion.

McDougal gave him a quick glance, hissing out a warning. "Don't let . . ."

He stopped speaking abruptly as the object on the left rose up. McDougal had his rifle to a firing position, but the big, black object issued an unmistakable bellow, and followed by its companion, bounded into the sea.

"Seals!" growled McDougal.

For a moment the men stood motionless, staring limply into the breakers at the vanishing forms, then resumed the march.

The seal incident had cost the adventurers precious time. They hurried on down the beach, less cautious about their tracks, and paying less attention to the shadows at the upper edge of the beach. Only when steeper slopes brought the water's edge close to the driftwood logs and misshapen trees that struggled among the sand hills did they carefully watch to shoreward.

More time passed—an hour or more. Mist had turned into light rain, cleansing the atmosphere of some of the low-hanging fog, improving visibility and making the shadows more distinct. During this interval the two men's spirits were lifted, but the effect was not to last. As the rain clouds thickened, the shadowy forms became less distinct. The men became more wary.

A low voice muttered, "How far do ye think we hae come, M'Dougal?"

"I don't know. I thought we would have sighted the headland in the distance by now, but it's too dark."

From somewhere beyond the dunes a dog barked. The adventurers had ceased talking, and were moving on in silence, but it was too late. The dog's keen ears had picked up strange voices, and it was intent upon making its discovery known.

The barking came closer. Soon it was even with them, unseen, in the shadows at the edge of the beach. A village must be nearby, though no lodges were visible, and no Indian voices were to be heard. The noisy mongrel persisted.

"Is it a village? I cannae see anything," came a muffled voice.

"One is bound to be just over the first dunes, M'Tavish. Those mutts aren't out here alone. Have caution."

"Should we run to pass quickly?"

"No, that would alarm it. Just keep going and ignore it."

The dog was behind them, but had become aroused by the discussion, quiet as it was. It came into view, out of the shadows, toward McDougal and McTavish, increasing the pitch of its barking. Another dog picked up the call, then other sounds from beyond the dunes —human voices. Indians.

"Run," growled McDougal, and the two sprinted forward.

The dog had routed its quarry, and was claiming the chase and the victory. Its voice was a frenzy as it charged down the beach feeling secure as the intruders showed their heels. The second dog had reached the beach, but hesitated there, waiting, perhaps, for its Indian masters.

"Keep close to the water," McDougal hissed. McTavish rushed on, making no response. He was behind, and the dog was closing on his ankles. It was a large, lanky brute, large enough to inflict a serious bite, and the Scot's thoughts were on what he should do if the animal attacked. He didn't want to fire a shot and wondered if the rain had dampened the priming in his rifle's pan. He could strike the dog with the butt of his stock, but it hadn't come that close yet. His attention diverted behind him, McTavish stumbled, took his eyes from the dog, regained his stride, and continued on.

For nearly a quarter of a mile the dog followed, still barking, but not attacking, finally dropping farther and farther behind. Surely, though, they must be out of sight in the darkness from the place where the Indians would have come upon the beach. The men slowed to a jog, then a brisk walk. The dog stopped barking, then disappeared from sight.

"A moment, M'Dougal. Let's give a listen," McTavish puffed.

It was difficult controlling their breathing long enough to study the night sounds well. Even when their breath was held, their heart's pounding masked other noises, save the roar of the breakers and the swish of waves over sand. By the time he had stopped puffing, McDougal was satisfied they were not being pursued.

"It is fine, M'Tavish. We are past them. They probably thought the dog was chasing some wandering deer, and have gone back to their beds." He looked down to see if his tracks were visible. They were not.

Fatigue had become a problem. Legs were tired from the unceasing walking, and running had exaggerated the aches and weakness. They must have been on their feet for at least four hours.

"My legs feel quite worn, M'Dougal. Is it nae time we rested and regained our strength?"

"No, we had best go on a bit farther in case some of the Clatsops cannot get back to sleep and decide to stroll out and find what the dogs chased up. Besides, if we walk onto the loose sand, we will leave tracks for them to find."

"All right, but we should find some way to rest soon," McTavish responded, and the brisk pace was resumed with McDougal still in the lead.

For the next half hour they continued in silence, hearing no other sounds than their own footfalls and the steady roar of the breakers. Occasionally groups of shadowy sandpipers would scurry along in front of them, or fly off to gain some distance, but they made no sound.

Then, off to the left, along the edge of the shadows, the men heard a noise. Something had upset a piece of driftwood and it had fallen with a clatter among the debris. They stopped, and peered into the darkness. There it was again. A low form passed rapidly along before the dunes, occasionally disappearing behind a driftwood log. Then it was gone.

The creature had not appeared human, but the men were more cautious, casting frequent glances shoreward and behind them, as well as ahead, as they continued.

A stream flowed lazily into the Pacific, a small one, making no barrier to the path along the beach. However, winter flooding had changed the pattern in the dunes, so that a valley was cut into the mounds of sand that lined the shore. Save for a few logs that stormy seas had deposited on the stream-bank, the little valley was clear.

As the men waded across the shallow stream, both partners kept a watch to see if the animal, or being, would show itself in the opening.

"That damned dog!"

Yes, the dog was accompanying them, caught up in the adventurous spirit of a trek along the shore, probably bored with the prospect of staying with its inactive, sleeping masters. It had chosen to follow the strangers.

"Well, at least it isn't barking."

"Aye, and it might even serve to warn us, should the need arise."

Relief felt, tension relaxed, the fatigue returned. Reaching the far edge of the stream, McTavish spoke again. "Let's rest for a bit. I have a thought.

"If we wade up the stream to yon logs we can sit upon them, then wade back doon to the surf. The waters will hide our passing as easily as the waves do."

"Yes, M'Tavish, that's a fine thought."

Wearily but cautiously, the two walked through the shallow water flowing across the sands. Upon reaching a log that lay alongside the stream, they sat down. McDougal picked up a piece of driftwood from behind the log, and laid it in the water, so they might rest their feet on something dry, while not moving out onto the sand.

"Do you have any idea what time it is, M'Tavish?"

The other man took out his watch, opened the case and looked closely, tilting the watch to capture some of the moon's light upon the face, but couldn't clearly make out the hands.

"I could nae make it out, but I think it is aboot one. We should hae four more hours of darkness. How far do ye make it to the headland?"

"Perhaps another four or five leagues; we are better than half way."

"Twelve to fifteen miles seems a long way, M'Dougal." It was difficult to see the expression on his face, but from the way his face hung, Duncan knew that McTavish was worried.

"It is going well, M'Tavish. We have enough time that we will have to stop and rest a wee bit more before it will be light enough to travel in the forest."

For a time the two sat in silence, then McTavish asked, "Are ye from the Highlands, Duncan?"

"Yes, though I have spent most of my life in Canada, and some years with the Americans. Most of my kin are at Inverey on the River Dee. They are of the Farquharson clan. One of my family was Alisdair M'Dougal. He was a great-uncle, I believe, who served closely with John the Third of Inverey."

"Aye, the Black Colonel."

"Then you ken my people."

"More the place, M'Dougal. Are ye familiar with the Warlock's Stone on the slopes of Craiglash?"

"I have heard of it. You are not a warlock are you?"

"Naye, M'Dougal, I am not a warlock, but I carry this chip of rock from the Warlock's Stone," McTavish answered, drawing from a leather pouch a pebble that, in the dim light, looked like so many others on the beach. "I think it is the stone that at times gives me, through dreams, some knowledge that is useful."

"What has it told you of our journey?" His voice sounded sarcastic.

"Nothing, McDougal. I cannae command it like a warlock. I have to wait and take what knowledge it brings to me."

Their discussion was interrupted by a noise in the drift nearby, and the men turned to see the Indian's dog poking about.

"Awa hame wi' ye!" snapped McTavish, standing up, sending the dog scampering off and signalling the end of the rest period. Then, in an apologetic tone, he added, "I would nae want to take the dog from its master."

Picking up the bit of drift upon which they had rested their feet, and tossing it back into the debris, McTavish took the lead back down the shallow flow, then south along the edge of the surf. The mist had stopped for the moment, and the light of the moon increased as thinner places in the fog passed overhead.

Another hour passed. They walked steadily in silence. The dog was nowhere to be seen, likely having returned to more familiar and hospitable surroundings. Ahead the horizon appeared darker.

They had come to a larger stream as McTavish dropped back to speak to his partner in a low tone. "It looks like rain ahead."

"It could be, but it might be the headland. This creek may well be the one where the Nehaynehum lodges are. If so, we are close to where we turn into the forest, but we had best be cautious. You may be right about this band being allied with the Killamuks."

Silent now, McTavish moved forward to resume the lead. Then both men steppedorward into the broad expanse of stream that faced them.

This was definitely a larger flow than they had faced before that night. Like the small trickles that crossed the sands, it was spread wide, but the volume was sufficient to erode some of the sand the waves of the sea had smoothed across the stream bed during high tide. Ahead of them was faster water, with still-shifting sand, then an island of beach which split the flow, and another broad expanse of stream.

McTavish started rapidly ahead, but suddenly found the sand sloping steeply, the waters up around his knees. The change caught him off guard, so that he nearly lost his balance, cursed softly, then stood erect. From then he moved slowly, intent upon pushing one foot then the other forward, keeping his legs spread wide for better balance. As the waters neared his waist, he lifted the thong on which his powder flask was hung, and held his rifle high above his head. He wondered how the shorter McDougal was faring, but dared not divert his attention to see.

On he moved, concentrating on the efforts. The current pressed steadily against his legs, sand washed away beneath his feet, and his buckskin trousers flapped in the flow so they beat upon his legs. It was only with the utmost concentration that he kept his footing and reached the island. With relief, however, he noted the portion of stream ahead was shallower and wider spread, so the current was not so intense.

McTavish turned to see how his companion was faring. He was nowhere in sight. Walking back to the edge of the temporary island, he studied the stream from whence he had come. Still there was so sign of McDougal, either in the water, nor on the bank beyond. Worried, he looked down the stream, toward the waves. Could he have been swept away?

Now he moved to the lower end of the island, where it was awash in the surf, and studied the waves. If the other man had been swept to sea, his form should appear in the breakers. John waded into the waves for a better look at the region where the waters of the stream and sea met. He could see nothing of his fellow voyager.

McTavish moved back up the sands, shoreward. He studied the shadows of the dunes and scrub trees, but could make out nothing in the darkness. Had a Nehaynehum arrow struck his companion down as he struggled in the stream? He didn't think so, for there were no sounds of alarm, and no other arrows from the shadows. He must have simply lost his balance and been swept to sea.

A tightening in his throat, the man considered what he should do. He could turn back and report the loss to the fort. No, that would serve nothing; they would be right back where they started, except one experienced man short. The apprentices would be more alarmed than before. No, he knew the plan as well as McDougal, and there was no evidence of Indian attack. He should go on alone.

McTavish's heart was heavy as he crossed the balance of the creek. Only at one point did the water reach his knees, and the skills he had learned earlier in holding himself steady in the current and shifting sands brought him through. As he stepped upon the solid beach, he raised his eyes. A shadow stood before him. McDougal!

"What happened to ye, mon? I thought ye drooned."

"When I saw the struggle you were having with the current I waded up the creek to where it was deeper but with less rush to tear at me. I got a bit wetter, and had farther to go, but ne'er lost my footing. I am afraid, though, that my powder flask got a wee bit damp."

Relieved, McTavish nodded, then headed on, walking briskly. Soon the shape of the headland became more and more distinct. The sands contained increasing amounts of pebbles, then larger rocks. For a while they could pick their way on the sands between the larger stones, but finally, as they neared the enormous rock cliffs that extended into the breakers, they found themselves struggling over large boulders.

"Come, M'Dougal, we hae come far enough. Let us make for the trees. We will hae to wait 'til dawn's light to make our way in the forest of the slopes, so we might as well get some rest."

Silently, the other complied, and the two climbed over the boulders, the logs cast high on the shore by winter storms, and to the very edge of the wall of thick thorny brush where mountain met the shore.

"One of us should stay awake, so I will take the watch," McDougal stated.

"No, I cannae sleep. Ye go ahead if ye can."

"In a bit perhaps; I'm not sleepy either."

For a time both men sat, resting upon the highest of the storm-tossed logs, partially hidden by vegetation, and looked out to the moonlit waves that pounded against the rocks, throwing plumes of bright spray high into the air.

"Ah, for a bit of Scottish whiskey to ward off this chill," muttered McDougal.

"I hae no whiskey left, but I brought along a bit of claret. Here, M'Dougal," McTavish replied, drawing a small flask from his coat and handing it to his companion.

"Ah, good," remarked Duncan, taking a large swallow and returning the flask. "Your clan is in the west of Scotland, isn't it?"

"Aye, most of the clan gathers at Sween Castle, but my family home is at Ardishaig on Lock Fyne." McTavish had never known his companion to be this friendly and wondered if it were the influence of the claret.

"The stronghold of the McDougals is a bit north of your clan, near Oban on the Firth of Lorn. They have never been too strong, though, caught up as they are between two groups of Campbells.

"'Tis odd, though, that my family would be across the Highlands with the Farquharsons.

"And, I have been wondering if that fellow, Lamazee, might have come from the clan that holds the lands between the Dee and Esk Rivers. You did know, didn't you, that his name is Ramsay, though he cannot pronounce it?"

"Ramsay, did ye say, M'Dougal?"

"Yes, when the filth is washed from his arm, and he has no garment over it, there is a mark upon him. 'Jack Ramsay,' it reads."

"Nay, I would think not, M'Dougal. But I ken some other Ramsays. I hae seen them several times as I traveled to London. Ye may hae known that I sought apprenticeship with Hudson's Bay though it ne'er was agreed upon.

"It was in a border village that I saw them, a poor bunch of tenants, most mean and low. The poorest of them lived in the village where they spent much of their miserable time in gaols and workhouses. At one time I believe I heard that some of their kind had gone to sea at early ages."

To his surprise John turned to discover McDougal fast asleep. For a while he sat lost in thought. The Clatsops, he mused, were not a war-like people though they did occasionally capture and keep slaves. He remembered that many of the Ramsays of the border village bore red hair, like Lamazee, and had their troubles with the King's law.

Was this one inciting the Killamuks to mischief? Lamazee hadn't appeared that contriving, but the men at the post had not really gotten to know him. Mostly, he stayed with the heathens, putting on trousers only when he came to the fort. However, he hadn't come to the fort in recent years, and the traders had only caught fleeting glimpses of him in the shadows of the forest.

If only his manners were not so strange. If it weren't for that, and for Lamazee's avoidance of contact with the traders, they might have been able to become friends.

What was it about his tongue? Was it just the impairment of speech, or did Lamazee speak English with a bit of Scottish, as someone from a border county might?

McTavish agreed with what Thompson had entered into the journal at the trading post. Yes, Ramsay was probably about thirty years of age. Donald McKenzie, there with the Pacific Fur Company before the purchase of Fort George, had stated that Lamazee was with the Neha-lems when the Astor party arrived in 1811 and understood that he had been seen by Lewis and Clark, the American explorers, when they reached the Pacific in 1805. It was too bad that McKenzie decided to leave with the Americans, for he had almost established a relationship with this strange redhead. For some unknown reason, Lamazee had been more willing to come to the trading post during its early days but had lost interest since the British acquisition.

John McTavish's thoughts continued to be of Ramsay as fatigue began to have its effect. He would, McTavish figured, have been only around twenty years of age when seen by Lewis and Clark but had already so thoroughly assumed tribal habits and spoke the native tongue so fluently that these men, though very familiar with the fron-tier, did not question whether Lamazee was, indeed, an Indian. So

Ramsay must have been quite young when he first came to this wilderness coast.

His eyelids were beginning to droop despite the wetness of his clothes as John's hand unconsciously drifted into the leather pouch, his fingers sliding around the piece of Warlock's Stone. Let's see. To have come here at that time, in the 1790s, Ramsay must have arrived in a ship drawn here by the sea otter trade. But McTavish knew of no English ship trading in this area though the King had given rights of English trade in this region to the Hudson's Bay Company around 1670. McTavish knew from his applications to that firm that they were nowhere near the Pacific shores and had no immediate plans to expand that far. Lamazee must have been with a crew of free-booters, a coarse lot that might have dealt a good deal of misery to such a lad.

John's eyelids closed, and his thoughts felt hollow as sleep overcame him. The Warlock's Stone was fast in his hand as McTavish slipped from consciousness into the dream world. Images drifted in, replacing the thoughts in his mind. His mind was clear, and vivid images were being built—as though by some strange force. Cold and anxiety were overcome, and John was floating away, called by other voices, to another land.

Two

The lines of buildings formed in the dark mist. The night was still, and a quay lined with taverns and ale houses interspersed with an occasional merchant's establishment lay beside the Tyne River. This was Newcastle. With the exception of the five-story structure of the "Gray Horse" tavern, the town was a crowded row of buildings, only two or three stories high, of Georgian and Stuart architectural style. Some were grey, others whitewashed, and many had been white but were now dismal from peeling and stains. No one was in sight. All was dark except for a single lantern that gave scant light to the cobbled street.

Unseen in the damp darkness, foot falls were heard as a group approached from the Side and onto Sandhill. This was the main road in from the Scottish border country.

Shadowy movement accompanied the footsteps, then silhouettes appeared in the dim light of the street lantern. Two men, large and bundled against the dreariness, came down the street. Between them was another form, identifiable as a young boy. Their silence suggested that this was not an amiable group, and the small lad seemed more to be under guard than escorted.

As they reached the quay, the little group turned broadside and proceded along the stone dock. Clacking of shoes on the cobblestones ceased as the men stepped upon the wooden buffers at the quay's edge. The three dark forms were moving toward a ship. Before them, in the fog, stood the black web of masts and rigging of a schooner.

The vessel, rising upon the waters of the incoming tide in the Tyne River, was a dismal-looking ship, its rigging black with tar, its hull and cabin also as dark as the coal of Newcastle. Somehow the colors of the new Union Jack occasionally reflecting the beams of the street lantern seemed out of place. Some other, darker flag would have looked more appropriate above the ship's stern.

They were close to the gangplank when the boy stopped walking and turned as though to run away. One of the men, walking so close that their shadows seemed to merge, sensed the boy's move and instinctively siezed him by the shoulder.

The silence of the night was broken by the coarse voice of a seafaring man. "Move, ye fool hare-lip. On wi' ye! Ye'r father warned me ye liked to run away."

The sounds echoed from the silent houses, but roused not a soul. The boy tried harder to twist away, and for his efforts received a stunning blow to the side of his head.

"I paid ye'r miserable family a sack of quid for ye'r services, and brought ye nigh from the border. Now ye are going to do the services I've paid for. Ye're not getting away from me now."

As they reached the narrow gangway, the other man, the one who had not spoken, dropped behind and kicked the boy in the rump as the first man half lead, half dragged his unwilling servant aboard.

Other shadowy forms appeared on the ship, but the night was still again. Silent forms moved down the gangway, spread out to the fore and after ends of the ship, then stopped. As though at an unheard and unseen signal, mooring lines were loosed and the plank hauled aboard. Shadows leaped back over the sides as dark masts slipped by the wharf. The tide-hastened river was carrying the ship away.

Sails were raised from the booms where they had been furled, and the skyline of Newcastle was disappearing in the background. Still, there was no sound—save the sobbings of a frightened boy.

And where was that English flag that had flown at the stern? All seemed dark and sinister now though sunrise was approaching.

Little was said to the boy as the crew quietly worked the vessel down the river. By the light of the sun, the masts seemed darkened by creosote or some other preservative, and not truly as black as they had appeared during the foggy night. Lines of the rigging were also stained by the soil and sweat of many hands and from the blotches of tar that had been carried from the stays and backstays. Other standing rigging was covered with serving and tarred, giving the area aloft the appearance of heavy black webs against the gray of the sails which now nearly matched the morning fog.

It was when the craft stood out to sea that misery and tension increased for the captive boy. Increasing winds blowing down the Channel caused the masts to move in their sockets with a groaning sound. Withes, the bands to which rigging was attached, seemed loose, having worn the masts beneath through long abrasion, and shifted with each tack. These unfamiliar sounds were frightening enough, but the

cers of the ship, became increasingly ill-tempered.

Noon approached, and Ramsay was dispatched below to bring lunch to his master's cabin. In the galley a stew was being prepared, a brown lumpy liquid that smelled strongly of cooking tomatoes, potatoes, and salted meat. The odor was distressing, and the boy's stomach was churning as he climbed the ladder from the galley. He knew he would vomit again.

Placing the bowl near the middle mast, he struggled to the rail to retch. However, by moving from the odor of the bowl of food and breathing deeply of the sea breeze, his nausea began to subside. For a moment he rested there, gazing back to where he imagined England lay, now out of sight, and waiting to see if he would retch over the side.

At that moment the officer appeared from his cabin, looking for his lunch. Spying it lying by the mast and his servant resting at the rail, he roared with rage. "So, ye be so'jering again. Ye obviously need a lesson in attention.

"Here, ye two sailors, secure this bilge-rat to the forward mast. He needs a taste of the lash."

Gleefully, the two men siezed the small form and dragged him forward. Stripping off his jacket and shirt, they placed his arms around the mast and tied his wrists. So small were his arms, and so large the mast, that he hung there pitifully, held up by the tightness of the ropes on the tapering mast.

The Ramsay boy gasped as the whip fell across his bare back. It hurt, and he could feel the sting where a row of red welts raised diagonally from his shoulder to his ribs. The second blow was even sharper, and the boy cried aloud. By now most of the crew had emerged from below and from their stations on deck. A roll of laughter responded to the cry.

The next stroke laid the whip across tissue that was already tender, and a scream ensued. The crew did not conceal their enjoyment of the torment, laughing and joking their approval. This encouraged more whipping, until the weakened body hung from the mast—a collapsed, crying child.

"Cut him down and have him fetch me that meal. It is getting cold." The punishment was over.

Cautiously and painfully, but as promptly as he could, the boy put his shirt and jacket back on. He could feel it sticking to his back where the whip had drawn blood.

To his master's satisfaction, the servant's promptness appeared to be improved. He forced his weakening body into spurts of energy whenever called upon to perform his errands. To ensure continued attention to duty, the officer occasionally rattled the handle of the whip against the cabin bulkhead.

The day ended terribly. Although he had been able to take some soup by evening, and was keeping it down, he was so tired and weak he could hardly stand. A hammock had been placed for him to sleep in near his master's cabin, but his back was too painful to lay on, and the sway of the hammock prevented him from sleeping on his stomach. Consequently, he found himself sleeping on his stomach on the deck. In this prone position, however, he was continually awakened by rats that ran across his face or nibbled at the dried blood on his clothing.

It seemed that the boy might not survive a third day at sea. From his location on the deck, he failed to hear his master's call and was starting the day lashed to the mast. This time he was too weak to cry out, to scream, or beg for mercy. He had given up all hope of living.

The lash was about to fall when a voice spoke up. "Wait, you are going to kill the boy that way."

"What do ye care? I paid for his service, and he isn't good for anything. Look. He will never be sturdy enough to serve at sea."

"Well, maybe I can use him ashore to help in the trading. How much did you pay for him?"

"Seven pounds, Mr. Smythe."

The newcomer's eyebrows raised, and he remained silent for a while, looking at the boy.

"Whatever caused you to take that much out of your purse?"

"Well, sir, he is to serve me for five years."

At those words the boy went limp at the mast, his head hanging so his matted red hair covered his face. He knew he would never see England and his family again—not that his family mattered to him. His drunken father had mistreated him, not wanting another mouth to feed and disdaining the boy's deformity. He ridiculed the fact that the lad couldn't pronounce the family name of Ramsay and roughly tatooed his name, "Jack Ramsay," on the boy's arm. Jack didn't want to die in this agonizing manner, though.

"Five years. I'll tell you, Roger. I will give you your seven quid, and he can serve me. A third mate doesn't need a servant anyway."

Roger Symington, the junior officer of the vessel, was haughty beyond his station, frustrated at not advancing in rank, but tight with what little money he did not squander in pleasures ashore. He looked down at the limp form still tethered to the mast, fingered his near-empty purse, then answered, "'Tis done, but ye won't get much work out of him."

With that, things became somewhat better. The sea had calmed over the previous days, and the boy's stomach settled. Smythe, one of the group of merchant venturers that owned the vessel, and the trader for this voyage, was less demanding that Symington. Jack Ramsay also became wise to the advantages of staying out of sight. His absences brought him a few floggings, but they were less severe than from his previous master, and the crew found less entertainment in them. Occasional floggings for absences were also better than being conspicuous and the constant butt of the crew's pranks.

Jack developed no friends among the men of the ship. He was, in fact, fortunate that the vessel was undermanned with only eleven men. Most of the time they had little time for mischief, certainly no time to hunt for an elusive little boy.

The incident that caused Jack to seek refuge in the very bowels of the ship, atop the damp stones of the ballast, occurred toward the end of the second week at sea. By this time the boy had recovered from his seasickness and was eating well—perhaps better than he had at home where there was seldom enough food to satisfy the needs of the family.

Jack had learned the routine of his new master. That is, he knew when he must be on deck and attentive and thus avoid a whipping. On this day he was scrubbing the deck of Mr. Smythe's combination office and stateroom (if anything on this dismal ship could be referred to as a stateroom). He had filled out sufficiently that his ragged clothes were now too tight, and as he bent over the rail, partially hidden by the longboat, drawing a pail of water, the seam of his trousers gapped open.

The youngster was intent on tossing the bucket forward and pulling at the proper moment so he did not see the rough sailor slipping up behind him, nor the wild look in the man's eyes. He was about to bring the bucket over the side when he was siezed roughly from behind and held, still bent over. Jack struggled to free himself from the crushing grip, and finally screamed in terror and pain. This, however, only brought a gathering of the sailor's comrades.

Jack pleaded, but to no avail. The man was having his satisfaction.

"You buggered him!" blurted out one of the late-arriving on-lookers. "What's the matter with you, Hugh? If Smythe sees you, he will go to the Captain, and you will be stretched on the yard boom."

"No, they're too short of hands to hang anyone from the cargo boom, not when we're this close to the Cape. In another day or two we will be battling the straits. Anyway, it didn't hurt him none."

"Yeah? But I don't think it wise to catch him right out on deck like this. Better find him below."

Jack, hurt and frightened, dashed below and hid. For the next few days he hid in the ballast, coming out only as he felt he must to tend to his master's chores and his body's demands. The sea was becoming rougher as time passed, however, with larger swells and sharp tacking that sent ballast stones rattling about. Jack was afraid that shifting rock might trap him in his dungeon.

He had little to worry about the crew, for they had their hands full on deck. Jack peered out onto a wind- and spray-swept deck, toward dark strips of hostile islands. Perhaps it was cold mixed with fear, but the chill seemed to pass clear through his body as he huddled at the rail.

Ahead, the seas were running higher, and a dark squall seemed to be sucking the craft towards it. Despite this approach of what seemed certain doom, birds were wheeling about, playing in the gusts of wind. Some were quite large, with wings spreading wider than the length of Jack's body. He heard some of the crew members call one of the birds an albatross and the abundant, smaller ones petrels.

None of the birds were menacing, but as the ship approached the storm and the winds mounted, more birds appeared. Jack listened to their cries, wondering what they meant. Could they be screaming a prophecy of doom for the frail ship?

The night was terrifying. Gusts of wind shrieked through the rigging, each one shaking the masts as though they would be torn from the deck. The groans and cracking of wood and fittings aloft were fearful. Jack slept little that night and wondered if the blackness would never end. What would happen if they were driven onto one of those jagged islands and cast into this icy, raging water?

The morning was not much better. The rain had lightened, and the wind was steady rather than in such destructive gusts. The Captain and one of the men stood looking up at one of the masts, inspecting it. There was some conjecture that the night squall had cracked it. At their feet lay some fallen rigging. Cautiously, one of the men climbed the swaying mast. Although it seemed he would be cast into the sea, he clung with numb hands as he followed the Captain's demanding instructions. No cracks were found, and in time they were satisfied.

Jack ventured to the rail as they approached more islands in a narrow strait. Fewer birds were about, but he was surprised to see a number of animals in the water. Most were seals, he thought, but others he surmised to be the sea lions the men were talking about.

Then the ship passed into an area of strong tides. Currents twisted this way and that, sending waves in all directions to buffet the ship. The boy grabbed the rail and gasped as cold spray leaped up the side to drench him. For an hour the ship was tossed about, then the effect subsided.

For two weeks the passage around the Horn continued, with the accompanying squalls, high seas, and strong currents. Then the ship slipped past all sight of land. The weather abated, all sails were hoisted, and life aboard ship returned to normal.

In the following months, Jack's terror shifted from the sea to the crew. One hiding spot after another was discovered until the boy found safety only when squeezed into the space over the ballast. Here he found a hole in which to hide whenever he felt pursued.

Then one day the ship dropped anchor in a small, shallow bay. The sounds of the sails being lowered and the kedge anchor being set enticed Jack out on deck. They were at an island in a strange land. The trees were not like any he had seen in England, and the mountains of the island rose sharply into clouds that hung about their tops. On the beach he could see long slender boats, and several more were in the water approaching.

Jack ducked below as two sailors approached and came face-to-face with Smythe, his master. Jack was quickly dispatched to the hold to fetch some nails, beads, and knives. He didn't know what they were intended for and was curious to watch. The opportunity was not immediately available, however, as Jack was again dispatched to the hold, this time for some colorful cloth.

When the boy returned with the cloth, he found that the people in the canoes had climbed aboard the ship. As he stepped onto the deck he was astounded to see three naked men, clad only in feathered head-dresses, their bodies decorated with tatoos. He stopped, his mouth open, and stared until Smyth called sharply, "Here, step lively! Fetch those things here."

Jack walked well around the savages to reach his master. He handed the goods to Smythe, and Smythe handed some of them to the strangers for examination. While the trader was so occupied, Jack had time to see what else was going on. The sailors were interested in something in the water beside the ship. Excitement was high, and no one turned to notice the boy.

Through a scupper Jack caught a glimpse of another canoe below the spot where the men were gathered. As he stepped to the rail, the heads of the crewmen were raising, and hands were eagerly reaching out. Onto the deck they helped several women.

And the women were naked! Jack had never before seen the body of a woman. Curiosity drew him closer as the men were enticing the women towards the open companionway. Jack wondered what the crewmen would do, and as excitement and anticipation overcame his fear of the men, he drew closer to them. He wondered what was going to happen and was totally unaware of the trading of goods for fresh fruits and poultry that was taking place on the other side of the deck.

"Sail!" The cry stopped all action for the moment. Symington, the junior officer, was the first to the rail. He didn't need a glass, for in their distraction, no one had seen the ship approaching until it was only a few miles away.

"She's a man-o-war, Cap'n! I can't see her colors, but she is a big 'un!"

The captain reached into his belt, seized his pistol, and fired it into the air. Natives dived overboard and swam to their canoes; crewmen rushed about getting ready to hoist sail.

"Get that anchor in, quick! You, there, start raising sail now! Ramsay, give them a hand at the capstan!"

Jack had never been called upon to serve this way before, and he felt honored though he feared the men he would work with. But this would give him a chance to prove his worth. He grabbed a belaying pin, struck it into a socket in the capstan, and began to push as he had seen the sailors do. Immediately he tripped over the line and nearly fell, receiving a growl of "Pick up yer feet." He did and struggled clumsily on. The anchor came aboard and was ready for tying in place when Jack again tripped over the line and fell. A kick to one side was his pay for seaman duty.

The black schooner was under way but gathering speed slowly. On came the other ship, bearing down on them. She was too far away for her cannon to be effective, but Jack saw a puff of smoke and heard a bang. He ducked behind the rail before he realized that it was only a signal. The warship wanted them to stop.

A chase was on. Ordinarily, the schooner would have been able to pull away from most full-rigged ships. However, the black schooner had not had her hull cared for since leaving Newcastle, and now she was burdened with a layer of seaweed. Her speed was reduced by the friction. The warship appeared to be gaining slightly, although it would probably take all day to reach cannon range. Then it would be over. The chase would end, and if they were not destroyed by cannon, they would be in deep trouble for not having yielded to the signal to stop. Jack wondered why they were avoiding a ship that might belong to the King of England. Perhaps he was with a band of pirates.

For hours the crew worked the dark ship, passing between islands and over the open sea between them. The last bits of land in the chain lay ahead, a long series of small islets with shallow water between them. Coral heads and rocks were close to the surface in many parts, as evidenced by discoloration in the water and turbulence where the reefs were closest to the surface. The captain studied the waters ahead. "Are ye thinking of trying to pass between?" Symington asked.

"We will have cannon shot around us within an hour if we don't. Just hope the captain of that man-o-war isn't feeling like risking his ship at the moment."

"Aye, Captain. She is a big 'un. I can see her colors now; she is British, though I don't make out the nameboards."

"All the more cause to take a chance on sinking. It wouldn't be worse than the execution dock.

"Keep a sharp lookout up there! Watch for shoal water! And Cavendish, get up to the bow and watch! We are passing through between the little islands!"

38

Jack stood at the rail, watching breathlessly. No one spoke. Roger Symington silently took the wheel from the helmsman and pushed the man aside. Symington was ostensibly the third mate, but there were no first or second mates; he was the only junior officer. This embittered him, but his reputation was such that no captain, and in particular not Captain Beasely, wanted to trust him with greater authority.

The relieved man, Andrew Bloar, came to the rail near Jack. He, like the other men, had offered no friendship to the boy, but he had been one of the least antagonistic. Jack decided to ask the question that was burning inside him. Gathering his nerve, he blurted out, "Why—why are we r-r-running from an English ship—sir?"

"We got no charter—the King's people ain't given permission for us to be here, kid. And they don't like tradin' wi'out the papers. They'd 'ang us all if they catch us."

Jack turned a little pale and placed a hand to his throat. He wondered if they would really hang a boy. His thoughts were on what he would tell the King's officers; he really didn't know what was going on, nor had he come by choice.

"Shoal water, dead ahead about a quarter!"

"How wide is it, Mister Arnold?"

"Not wide, sir. About twice the width of the ship, but there is more white water beyond."

"Do you make the water better to port or starboard?"

"Starboard looks better, sir."

"Ten degrees to starboard!"

"Aye, aye." Captain Beasely, unaware of the switch at the wheel, turned and scowled at Symington but said nothing. Instead, he walked aft to see what the warship was doing.

"Ah, she's taking in sail."

The dark ship passed the submerged rocks, then slid into water so shallow that coral heads could be seen jutting up from a sea-floor composed of shells, sand, and broken coral. All sails were still up, and the lookouts on the mast and at the bow were nervously trying to pick the calmest and, hopefully, the deepest, waterway.

Behind, the warship had turned broadside. Several puffs of smoke signaled the firing of cannon. Symington had glanced back and noted this development. "Shall we alter course to dodge 'er shots, Captain?"

"No." There was no explanation, but Captain Beasely seemed to know that his ship was too far away for the gunners to be aiming accurately. Any hit would be pure luck.

A geyser of water erupted astern. Swishing sounds caused the crewmen on deck to duck low, for the sound announced that the next cannon balls would be reaching farther. Another geyser shot up off the port bow, then another far to starboard.

No more cannon were fired. They had reached the limit of their range. The only hazard now was the dangerous waters. By the time the warship could circle the string of islands and pick up chase again, night would be closing in. The black vessel would slip away in the darkness.

"Blue water ahead, sir! We're clear!"

The ship was quiet that night, though the course was altered twice in case they were being pursued. As soon as daylight arrived, Captain Beasely ordered a boat lowered and towed along side. Two men with long-handled scrapers and brushes worked all day on the sides of the ship to reduce the amount of seaweed that clung to the ship's hull. Few barnacles needed to be removed as those that collected in the colder climate had dropped off, and the new ones from the warmer sea were still small.

For the next few months they were sailing across open sea. Water had to be rationed, and the provisions were stale, some spoiled. They were terrifying months for Jack. Months during which irritated and frustrated seamen sought satisfaction with him. Jack spent considerable time squeezed into the hole over the ballast. Large rats were his companions, but they were less threatening than the crew.

Then one day the ship dropped anchor in a small, shallow bay. They were in a strange, wild land, heavily forested with tall green trees. Some of the men went ashore, but the others remained aboard at all times. Weapons were carried, for they did not trust the natives.

It was a calm day, with none of the sea mists that frequently cloaked this coast. The tall green fir trees of the immense forest stood stark still, and in the clear air the sharp peaks of the mountains just beyond the steeply rolling coastal hills stood out silhouetted against the blue sky. It was a scene that roused the spirits of venturesome souls.

Remembering the naked women in the islands they had visited piqued Jack's curiosity about the natives. He found himself on deck, trying to remain obscure in a corner as he stood looking in awe at the unbroken wilderness. He had no idea that trees could grow so tall or so dense. There had been sharp peaks of mountains to be seen when they passed the cold region of islands and mountainous headlands when they had rounded the straits, but he had been too cold and frightened of the storms to study them.

Now Smythe and the captain were ashore. Symington was in charge of the vessel when Hugh, Jack's original sexual assailant, chanced to spot the small form by the rail. With a malicious twinkle in his eye, he motioned to two of his cronies nearby and began to slip toward Jack. The others joined in, and began to draw a circle about their intended victim. Closer they crept until escape was sealed off. One of the men could contain himself no longer and let out an evil laugh.

Jack whirled, looking into the grinning malicious faces. He darted along the gunwale, but was cut off by the quick steps of one of the men. Doubling back rapidly, he tried to outrun another near the stern castle. He was cut off again. Three burly, smelly men were closing in. He looked around the deck and saw Symington turning the other way. Jack knew there was no help.

A rough hand siezed him, lifted him off his feet, and turned him around. Another hand clamped around his midsection.

Three

"M'Tavish!" Hands shook his shoulders as the harsh whisper broke through the cries of terror in his dream. He almost slipped off the log on which he was resting, but his hands instinctively clutched at irregularities on the wet surface. "It's light, and there are people on the beach!"

"Oh, I'm sorry. I did nae intend to fall asleep," McTavish muttered softly. He siezed up his rifle and looked intently along the rocky beach before him. A solitary dog stood on a rock near the edge of the water, looking at them, but making no sound.

Voices came from the beach to the north. A group of Indian children were approaching. They were intent upon keeping their footing as they crossed the slippery rocks.

Suddenly another dog, the one that had followed the two men, appeared beside them and began barking at the dog on the beach. McDougal siezed a club of driftwood to silence the dog, but McTavish moved quickly to stop him. McTavish slipped on the damp logs, and a rotten limb clattered down through the driftwood. John regained his balance, and the two men reached the mass of brush that marked the dividing line between the rain forest and shore. They broke into the tangle and began scrambling through, the bushes scratching at their faces and clothes. Despite their struggle, they made little progress. John glanced back. The dog on the beach was walking toward them, and two of the children were standing near the dog—watching. They had been seen.

The mat of brush, with its hundreds of tiny, sharp spines, soon thinned, but the needles of the stunted spruce trees at the edge of the forest replaced them. At least they could move faster in the low-growing trees.

"Where do we go from here?"

"We climb onto this slope, find a game trail, and follow it along the stream until we locate a pass south through the mountains."

"Is this the stream where that group lives that might be a band of Killamuks—what are they, M'Dougal, the Necanicums?" Knowing

McDougal's temper, he was hesitant to mention the fact that they had been seen. The knowledge should make little difference in the travelers' caution or speed; it would only increase the pressure. McTavish was counting on the time it would take for the children to return to the village and sound an alarm and for a party of braves to come looking for them. He hoped that they would have a good head start before then.

"I think they are called the Nehaynehum, but their village is up the stream. We will avoid them."

These words partially reassured McTavish, for if the children were from a village by the shore, they would be Clatsops and less likely to bring an attack. If they were Killamuks, they would have had a greater distance to travel to their village to spread an alarm, and pursuers would have farther to go to pick up the white men's trail.

With that brief exchange of words, the two men climbed through the small trees along the top of the sloping bank and broke into a tall, dense rain forest. For a distance of nearly a hundred yards they struggled with small trees, clumps of bushes, sturdy vines, and an entangling litter of fallen limbs. At times their footing was hidden by thick growths of ferns and they slipped and tripped many times.

To their relief, beyond the thick border of the forest, they emerged beneath huge trees that reached tall and straight toward the sky, clean of limbs below the lofty branches that joined together high above like a cloud-sifting ceiling. In the twilight below, vine-like bushes grew, their twisting trunks garlanded with moss. Since the forest floor was carpeted solely with low-growing ferns and holly-like plants, the adventurers were able to see ahead for several hundred yards at a time. Except for the huge, decaying logs that they were occasionally obliged to climb over, they found traveling relatively easy.

McTavish followed McDougal as they traversed the north side of the mountain. Occasionally he glanced back but saw no followers. He felt certain that any person traveling at this pace would be obliged to walk upright and would be seen. He frequently looked down and attempted to return to normal any ferns they had disturbed and hid leaves that had been torn from the vine-like bushes as they passed. He was not experienced enough to catch every twig and bit of moss, though, and was certain that an expert tracker could follow them. It was comforting to know that the coastal Indians were dependent on fish and mussels and were not the accomplished hunters and trackers that the forest tribes were.

It was not long before the two were more at ease under the canopy of mammoth evergreen trees. Silence reigned. The moist litter of needles from the branches far above absorbed the pounding of their hurried steps. Even the dead twigs on the trail, softened by the morning mist, bent with their weight, seldom snapping. Ferns and bushes became less dense so it was possible to avoid turning leaves, crushing ferns. They left few tracks to follow.

In this silence of undisturbed passage, McTavish had an opportunity to think back on the vision of the night before. He had no doubt that his dream was influenced by the warlock's stone which was now back in its pouch.

His thoughts were interrupted by McDougal's voice. "Shall we stop and eat a bite?"

"Aye." McTavish now realized that he was hungry—that they had not eaten since leaving Fort George. It seemed peaceful enough for a meal. Even the sounds of their voices were absorbed in the softness of the woodland.

Seating themselves on a convenient log, the two removed dried meat from their packs and began to gnaw ravenously at their leathery, meager meal.

"I wonder if these blue berries are fit to eat. Have ye ever tried them?" McTavish asked.

"Yes, I have. They are rather tasteless, but I suppose they would suffice this morning." With that comment McDougal knelt down and began to pick some of the small clusters of round berries from a ground-dwelling plant with rounded, dark-green leaves. "They remind me of blueberries, but they don't have near the taste. The Indians will eat them, but only if they don't have huckleberries and blackberries."

"M'Dougal, I had an interesting dream last night as we rested at the edge of the beach. In it I saw a wee lad being taken aboard a dark vessel and held in servitude. I think it might explain how Lamazee came to be here—"

McDougal was about to give a caustic response, when he turned suddenly to look back the way they had come and raised his hand abruptly. For several minutes they stood, listening and watching, as

McTavish nervously fingered the hammer of his rifle. At one moment McTavish thought he saw movement among the low-growing ferns, but it did not seem to be moving upright like a human. Then all was silent and still—it must have been his imagination.

"Perhaps we had better move on," said McDougal in a low voice.

"Aye," responded McTavish, adding, "I have a feeling the children on the beach saw us." McDougal ignored the statement, but McTavish felt better after the confession.

Taking care to make their passage noiseless, Duncan McDougal led the way again, moving along the hillside. They had come upon a game trail, a pathway of countless deer and elk, and their movement was now less impaired. They were making good progress now by virtue of the improved pathway and the fact that they were not climbing as steeply as they had been. The elk trail passed around the mountain in a very gradual ascent.

They continued on the trail for an hour or more. McTavish frequently glanced back and occasionally thought he saw a shadow moving across the path, but he heard no sounds, and any shorter-legged Indian pursuers would have had a difficult time keeping up with this pace and staying concealed. His eyes were deceiving him, he assured himself, confusing him by attributing movement to dissolving wisps of fog in the shadows of the trees.

Suddenly, McDougal raised his hand again. McTavish stopped and listened, watching carefully behind, ahead, and to the sides. Duncan stealthily left the path and began descending the slope.

McTavish placed his thumb on the hammer of his rifle and waited. Mentally, he selected a large decaying log to take cover behind, but he neither heard nor saw anything hostile.

Presently McDougal returned to the trail and said in a low voice, "I heard voices ahead."

"What do ye make of them?"

"We have not climbed sufficiently following this game trail. The creek is just below us, and the voices are across the creek."

"Aye, but who?"

"It sounded like children. We may be close to the lodges of the Nehaynehum. Let's be quiet and leave this path. We must climb higher on the hillside."

McTavish nodded.

Taking extra pains to make their passage noiseless, McDougal led the way around trees and logs, following deer paths whenever they ran higher up the slope as the two men moved eastward paralleling the route of the stream. As they progressed, they heard voices again. This time McTavish clearly heard them and agreed that they were, indeed, children at play. Other voices were also heard, adult voices, but below them and down the slope. These seemed to be coming from the creek, perhaps Indians fishing for trout. The sounds were peaceful, suggesting that this village, at least, was unaware of the intruders.

They crossed a ridge that dissected the slope and entered a draw that carried spring water to the stream below. The voices of children at play and even the fishing party at the creek were drowned out by this barrier, the sounds lost among the ferns and mosses of the trees.

Ahead, in the moist draw, the underbrush thickened, making passage over the soggy ground difficult and slippery. McDougal stepped up onto a decaying log in an attempt to avoid the seeping water under foot. His moss-covered footing gave way and his left leg slipped down the trunk, tearing away a large red section of the rotten log. He grasped for something to break his fall, but the slender bushes within his reach were too small. They only served to twist his body so he fell on his back rather than his side. He lay ignominiously on the forest floor, still clutching a handful of torn shrubs.

Twenty feet beyond, in the cover of the draw and just beyond their range of vision, came a crash, then a thump. Had Indians crossed the stream and moved in ahead of them? Was this an ambush? McTavish stepped behind a tree and braced his rifle against the trunk, waiting for the onslaught. McDougal crouched behind the log, fumbling with his weapon and unslinging the powder horn and shot bag which had become twisted behind him when he slipped.

Another thump, farther up the hill and to their right. And was that another sound behind them? McTavish started to look behind, then his eyes caught the movement above and ahead of them. A grey sleek form went gliding between the trees, thumping as it jumped an occasional log—a deer. It appeared to be a large buck, its antlers still thickened by unshed velvet.

Yes, there was another sound behind them, and now somewhat up the slope. McTavish turned his attention in that direction just in time to see a large dog heading off in pursuit of the buck. His eyes had not deceived him—they had been followed. It was the same dog that had followed them on the beach the night before and revealed their presence by barking that morning.

McDougal sat upright, then regained his footing, watching the animals disappear.

"Are ye all right, Duncan?"

"I seem to have disturbed my left ankle a bit, but I think it will soon pass. We had best move out of here."

"Aye, if yon mongrel has brought his Indian masters, I would rather be out of this brushy draw, the better to see them."

More cautiously, somewhat more slowly, the two continued across the draw and along the slope beyond. McDougal was limping, but they were making steady progress away from the Indian camp. They had passed undetected despite their clumsiness.

It was nearly mid-day when the travelers stopped again. They sat upon a fallen tree in an open portion of the forest. The dog, since he had been seen, made no effort to conceal himself upon returning from his futile chase of the deer.

"What shall we do about the dog, M'Dougal?" asked McTavish as Duncan drew a portion of dried meat from his pouch for a noon meal.

"Couldn't we drive him off?"

"I do nae know, but I would rather he were with us than prowling about we know nae where." McTavish had also drawn out some dried meat and tossed a piece in the direction of the dog.

The animal started, then sniffed the air and slowly walked toward the morsel. Gulping it, he tucked his tail between his legs and slunk to within a few feet of McTavish. John tossed the dog another morsel and finished his own lunch.

"Well, Duncan, we appear to have gathered in a stray, something of a fellow roamer."

"You have," McDougal grumbled.

"We do nae have enough food to keep feeding you, Roamer, but ye are welcome to travel with us." Responding to the tone of McTavish's voice, the dog moved closer, his tail wagging.

McDougal grunted, then commented, "At least if we run out of food we can eat your friend. No doubt that's what would have happened if he had remained with the Clatsops."

McTavish rose, signalling that they should resume the journey.

47

John took the lead, and Duncan, still favoring his left leg, fell in behind. Roamer, having gained some confidence, leaped ahead.

By late afternoon the party was forced to descend the slope. The steepness of the hillside they were traversing and its effect on McDougal's ankle was one consideration. Another, and more pressing, was the openness of the cover and thickness of the brush they were encountering. The trees of this part of the forest stood tall and starkly limbless, blackened in places by some past fire, but mostly whitening in death. Across the stream the trees were still green, spared by the fire that had ravaged this side.

Since they could easily be seen in the burned area, they decided to move north across the creek and continue up the valley along the opposite slope. Where they crossed, a smaller stream joined with the one they had been following.

"Duncan, are ye sure it would nae be best to turn and follow this wee creek into the mountains to the south?"

"No, I don't think we have traveled far enough inland to bypass the Tillamook Mountain and Neahkanie. If we cross the main stream and continue up this valley, staying part way up the other ridge, we can see the south. The clouds are breaking up, and by nightfall we may be able to calculate our best crossing over the mountains."

Ver-ry well, if it gae us a pathway out of these brambles."

They had come into a patch of thorny bushes much like those that had scratched them as they left the seashore. Nearing the stream, they used the steep slope to advantage, pushing down mats of bushes that already leaned and walking over them. It was a relief when they finally broke out into the shallow, clear water flowing over a smooth gravel streambed. Along this wet path the travelers walked for nearly a quarter of a mile until faced with a hole too deep to wade, and terminating in rushing cascades at its upper end.

Here they stepped out onto moss-covered rocks beneath white-barked, broad-leaf trees. Beneath the trees berries grew on slender bushes.

"These are unusual," McTavish commented, picking one. "Somewhat like raspberries, but much paler in color. Quite tasty, though."

"These are the ones the Clatsops gather to make some of their dried berry preserve, the kind that looks like leather. In their language they call this the salmon berry." McDougal sat down on a rock to empty the stream water from his boots.

It was then that McDougal discovered his ankle was badly swollen. Puffy and red in places, it still showed a white indentation where he poked it with his finger. McTavish came over and sat down beside him, looking down with a frown. "Do ye think we hae best stop?"

"It looks bad, but it hasn't been hurting that much. I would rest more comfortably if we got a bit farther from the lodges of the Nehaynehums before we camped."

"It would probably help if we bind it. Here, let me carry yer pack and rifle."

"I would rather keep my rifle close, but I think I will cut me a walking stick." With this, McDougal selected one of the vinelike bushes and cut a sturdy shaft from its trunk. He retained his rifle, but agreed to let McTavish carry both packs.

McDougal stumbled as the march resumed and limped more than prior to the rest stop. "It will take a while to get it limber again," he said, but McTavish was doubtful.

They had moved about a hundred feet from the stream when John stopped. Before him was a trail. "What do you make of this, Duncan?"

"I would say this is an Indian trail. Over there, see, are some moccasin tracks in that damp spot." McDougal hobbled over and knelt down to examine the tracks.

"Well?"

"It was a small group and probably went up the trail this morning."

"A war party?"

"Probably not, although they could have been scouts. There aren't enough for a serious attack. I only made out five sets of footprints."

"Hae we better move on up the hillside?"

"No, perhaps not. The trail doesn't look like it has been used much recently, and this group is small enough that I don't think they will be too bold. We can be on guard for an ambush.

"The trail will be faster and much easier walking. We can be careful to leave no tracks, going around the muddy places and dusty parts of the path."

"Aye, it would be better for your foot, too."

"Let's follow it then, but wait a moment while I check the priming in my rifle. I had better take my pack, too, in case we get separated in a fight."

Satisfied that their powder was still fit, the men began to ascend the trail carefully. They continued for nearly an hour, peering cautiously around each bend, listening periodically for any sounds, and constantly mindful not to leave tracks.

In time the trail came to an opening, an area on the north side of the stream where fire had scoured the forest. Here the path broke off into many trails, winding about clumps of luxuriant bushes. Trees either stood dead and starkly naked or with life only in clumps of green limbs near their tops. Deer and elk tracks obscured the marks left by moccasins.

Across this wide, bushy meadow moved the travelers, now walking abreast.

"Who caused this tremendous fire, M'Dougal?"

"The Indians. They burn the trees off so the berry bushes will grow."

The two men separated momentaily, going to each side of a bush that stood in the way. At that moment, McTavish realized they were not alone. He heard voices on the other side of the bush. Stopping to listen, he could make out that one speaker was an Indian—and the other was McDougal! Cautiously John moved around the bush, his rifle ready. Just a few more steps and he would have a clear view.

McTavish found himself in a passageway between clumps of huckleberries. There before him stood his partner, McDougal, talking with a young Indian woman. Taller and more slender than most Indian women he had seen, she was indeed a handsome sight standing there in the warm sunshine of the hillside, barebreasted and clad only in a skirt of reeds. Long black hair, well oiled and shining in the sun, flowed down and over her shoulders. For a moment McTavish stood speechless, admiring the smooth brown skin and graceful lines of her body.

Then a small child came toddling from the far patch of brush. "Come, M'Dougal, we hae best not leave any trouble to plague us on the pathway back."

McDougal uttered a word of Clatsop, then turned and walked toward McTavish. "Here, John, carry my pack again if you will."

"Is your leg worsened?"

"No, but we need not fear from any of the group that came up this pathway."

"No?"

"No, they are just a group of squaws gathering berries."

As if to give credence to McDougal's pronouncement the distant cry of a baby was heard, coming from the direction of the other berry pickers.

They pushed on. With the relaxation of tension, however, came the awareness of fatigue and hunger. The salmon berries and bits of jerky had not served long in place of a lunch, and it had been a day and a half since either had enjoyed any real sleep.

They passed the burn and re-entered the forest. The Indian trail had not resumed. Apparently it only went as far as the berry fields. A game trail served for a while, but the traveling was becoming more arduous.

"Let's go up into the timber on that next ridge and find a resting place."

"Do ye think it is safe yet?"

"I think so, M'Tavish. Besides, we would do better at defending ourselves if we were not so tired."

"Aye, ye are probably right."

As they crossed the next draw and climbed the other slope, each step seemed to be harder than the one that preceded it. Duncan McDougal was favoring his leg more, and he was becoming impatient with his walking staff. When they reached the concealment of the thicket, they were quite ready to sit down. McTavish took out his watch, opened the cover, and looked inside. It was four o'clock.

For a few minutes both men sat in silence eating dried meat and sipping from their canteens. Roamer sat, looking hopeful, and catching an occasional tidbit tossed by McTavish. McDougal looked disapprovingly but said nothing.

Then the need for rest overcame the craving for food, and they lay back. McTavish was quickly asleep. McDougal fought back the drowsiness for a while, feeling that one of them should remain on watch. Before long, though, he too was dozing.

This time both men fell into dreamless sleep. Their bodies and their minds were too tired from the walking, the climbing, and the anxieties of the past night and day to expend any energy even in illusion.

Four

McTavish woke with a start. Something had fallen nearby; now another object dropped onto the debris of the forest floor a few feet down the slope. Roamer was awake but still lying at the base of a tree. The dog looked intently down the slope though he didn't seem alarmed. Of course, he was an Indian dog. Were his masters approaching?

"M'Dougal," John spoke lowly but sharply, placing one hand on his partner's shoulder as he raised his rifle with the other.

"Hm-mf. What is it?"

Duncan's voice was louder than McTavish would have liked, and its loudness caused an uneasy feeling in John's stomach. "There is something down below in the timber."

Again something crashed into the dead limbs that cluttered the ground. Both men eased into sitting positions, readying their weapons. They waited and listened.

Duncan followed Roamer's gaze as the dog tilted its head and looked up into the trees. They saw a small object drop to the ground and bounce down the slope. All eyes turned to the treetops. Yes, there it was. A furry form darted along a branch, reaching the end where it swayed precariously before unleashing another missile.

"'Tis just a squirrel, M'Tavish. Look, there it is, cutting the cones so it can gather the seeds for its winter food supply."

For several minutes the two men and the dog sat watching the squirrel in silence. Then McDougal asked, "What time is it?"

McTavish fumbled in his pocket, produced his watch, and responded, "Almost five o'clock. What say ye, Duncan, shall we camp here for the night?"

"No, with the sky clear I think we should climb up the ridge to get our bearings. It may be foggy again in the morning, so we should scout our path and plan our march while we are able."

"I do nae know, M'Dougal. That ankle looks quite swollen. I think it would be best if ye rested it."

McDougal extracted another piece of jerky from his pack and

placed one end of the strip in his mouth. Roamer rose up with a look of anticipation, but he didn't approach.

Duncan frowned as he pulled hard, trying to bite a chunk from the hard substance. It broke with a snap, and he settled back to chew and to think about their situation.

"Are ye thinking we should move higher in case the squaws alarm the braves in the Nehaynehum village?"

"No. They seemed surprised and curious but not hostile. Besides, they would be just reaching the village about now, and by the time warriors returned, it would be dark. These Indians prefer to fight from their canoes, and if they must fight on land, they do so in the daylight. We should be safe here until morning—but we should leave early."

It was McTavish who broke the silence again. "Why do ye nae rest a wee bit while I scout the high country. I will get our bearings and return. It should nae be necessary for both of us to climb the hill."

"Yes, that sounds reasonable."

John shouldered his powder horn and shot pouch, picked up his rifle, and surveyed the hillside he was to climb. "I donae guess I will need the pack. I will leave it wi'ye, Duncan."

As he pushed the bag closer to Duncan, the surly man scowled and turned to look at the dog which had raised up and was approaching slowly. "Why don't you take that cur with you for company, M'Tavish. I can do without him."

"Fine," John replied, motioning to Roamer. The dog responded and fell in behind his adopted master as the tall Scot started up the hillside.

McTavish felt refreshed after his nap. He was surprised how comfortably he climbed without the weight of his pack. It had been on his back for nearly a night and a day, and he had forgotten what it was like to walk without it.

The timber on this slope was mixed old growth and regrowth, the result of the spotty burning of some forgotten fire. The spaces beneath the old trees were fairly open, but clumps of young trees and brush obscured the view beyond each patch of old-growth timber. For a mile or more McTavish angled up the ridge, then crossed a flat area that held berry bushes but was now shaded by growing trees which inhibited the huckleberries from flourishing and producing many berries.

At the other side of the bench, the slope began again. Man and dog continued to the crest of the ridge, then followed the ridge eastward, still heading into higher country. Further inland, John could occasionally catch a glimpse of a high, rocky peak. He wondered if this could be the Neahkanie Mountain. It didn't appear to be in the right place according to their crude map and the information gleaned from the Clatsops.

If that *was* the Neahkanie Mountain, they were lost, at least in regards to their search for the Nehalems. He was confident that they could slip back to the fort, but their time and effort would have been wasted. They would also have reduced the strength of the fort needlessly. How were Frazer, M'Gillivray, and the others faring without their direction and assistance?

A thought brought cold chills down McTavish's back. He didn't believe that they had been followed. Certainly they had not been attacked. What if the Indians were watching, had seen the two most experienced frontiersmen leaving, and were now besieging the fort. He envisioned them making their way back to the post and finding a smoldering ruin. They, and the returning traders, would be vulnerable in this hostile land and would have to make a difficult fall and winter retreat across the mountains. John was beginning to feel that this expedition was folly—and very risky.

Ahead was a rocky outcropping, extending above most of the trees. If he could climb onto that, perhaps he could make out their location. McTavish headed straight for the barren point.

On reaching the rocks, he found the walls were not as solid as they had first appeared. Instead, fissures filled with brush-covered earth provided narrow passages to the top. He selected the one with the least brush and began his climb. To his relief he discovered a game trail that parted the brush as it weaved back and forth through the break. It was a narrow one, made by deer, perhaps, but more likely the regular path of smaller animals. As McTavish pressed through the brush of the narrow, steep canyon, he was often obliged to proceed on hands and knees and at other times to thrust his weight against the brambles. "Aye," John muttered, "these stickery things are surely the devil's own clubs." He wished he could pass through as easily as did Roamer.

In time, the crevice narrowed and became shallower with only low-growing junipers and grasses, then failed, leaving the climber to crawl cautiously up a rock face.

As the rock flattened near the top of the outcropping, John emitted a sigh of relief and walked easily to a secure spot. Ahead of him, to the northeast, stood the barren top of a high rocky peak, its lower slopes green with small trees, berry bushes, and patches of brambles. Trails crossed the mellow fields, along one of which followed, in single file, a herd of elk. He stopped to count them, thirty-eight animals in all. If this was Neahkanie Mountain, it certainly was impressive.

Finally turning to look out into the direction from which he had struggled up the slope, he was quite unprepared for the panorama that lay before him. To the west and slightly south stood even more spectacular, sharply rising jagged peaks. These must be the dwelling place of the gods, the mountains the Indians call Neahkanie. Sharp and imposing rock pinacles rose above solidly forested hills, extending into the fluffy tufts of misty white clouds. Fog was beginning to form among the peaks.

To the left of the mountains, south of them and far below, the evening sunlight glistened on a large body of placid water. It was much like a lake, bordered by curving green slopes to the north, south and east. John knew this must be the estuary of the Nehalem River because the shimmering body was dissected from the wave-roughened expanse of the Pacific Ocean by a narrow line of land.

Before him, stretching out to the peaceful waterway, lay a gentle valley. John McTavish sat down and absorbed the quiet and peace of the scene before him. They were not lost, and for the moment he felt that the balance of the trip would be easier.

His spirits lifted, McTavish left the viewpoint and sought the way back down the bramble-filled defile. Most of the way back was downhill. It should be easy enough to return before darkness.

In the gloom of the forest, McTavish's senses returned to reality, and he moved cautiously. At last he reached the spot where he had left his companion. He found the marks left by a reclining McDougal, crushed ferns an indentation in the decaying forest floor. But where was McDougal? John readied his rifle and studied the trees, the fallen logs, and the thickets of small trees that were competing to fill the gaps where the forest giants had fallen. Shadows lengthened as the sun neared the tops of the ridges to the west. Wisps of ocean fog were beginning to drift between the trees.

Seeing no hostile movement, he called softly, "M'Dougal!"

"Over here."

Now, in a thicket in the direction of the returning voice, McTavish made out the blue of smoke mingling with the white mist of the evening.

"I have fixed us a shelter. What did you find?"

"I see that ye have. But are ye mindful of the savages? They aren't all as soft and bonnie-looking as the lass ye were talking to this afternoon. I am nae so sure we should show a fire."

"I have it in a hole behind the log—and we'll let it burn down before it gets dark enought for the glow to be seen. And don't worry about the Nehaynehum girl. She was very friendly."

"So I noticed. Illchee would have been very jealous."

"T'would be her misfortune."

"M'Dougal, I think ye a fortunate man to have a wife to care for ye out here in the wilderness. Ye're the only man at the post wi' a warm bed."

"She isn't that much of a bargain. First, her relatives would have emptied the warehouse, and now that Henry and you have put a stop to that, she sides with her father in chiding me for not having fought you and the whole bloomin English navy.

"They cannot seem to see that the Pacific Fur Company was about to go broke anyway. Mr. Astor was fortunate to be able to sell.

"But what did you learn on your trek? Did you find out anything?"

"Aye, ye can see clear to the land of the Nehalems from yon mountain. If we bear sou'east across the creek and over the far ridges, we will come to a glen that leads to the Nehalem land. It shouldn't be more than a day's journey."

"You could see the place?"

"Aye, we hae come far enough that one can see the Neahkanie mountains to the west and the valley of the Nehalems just to the south of them. The bay and valley are too large to be anything else unless we have gone so far that I was looking into the vast bay where the larger band of Killamooks live.

"And everything looked peaceful ahead."

"Caution, McTavish. Don't believe too much in just what you can see—particularly from that far away."

Their attention was drawn for a moment to Roamer, who came nosing in closer to the campfire. "I see you still have that Indian dog following you around. He'd better not get too close to me or we will have some fresh meat to cook on this fire."

The two men sat eating berries that McDougal had gathered, but their meat for the evening was their usual fare of dried jerky. They discussed the tensions that had prompted the trip. The Chinooks and McDougal's wife had done little to help. They talked of their having been seen by the Nehaynehum berry pickers and what that might bring.

In time McTavish told his companion about the previous night's dream.

"It does seem reasonable that he came here by ship. That is a most logical conclusion. But that does not mean that any dream of yours is the truth. And how did he become separated from his shipmates and end up living with the Indians?"

"Tha' is a good question. There must be some mischief in his history or Lamazee would have told us about it himself. Perhaps someone at Nehalem village will be kind enough to tell us."

"Perhaps he escaped to the village before the ship sailed."

"No, I think it would have been much worse. I cannae help but suspect some terrible mystery."

"Now, M'Tavish, do not get carried away with these mysteries and witchcraft. It may seem logical, but what you had was just a dream."

McTavish didn't respond though he clutched the warlock's stone briefly. He knew better.

The two sat in silence, staring at the fading embers of their little fire. It no longer gave much heat, but it had helped them dry out and put warmth into their bones. They lay back and fell asleep. No attempt was made to post a watch. Travel by night in the thickets of the western forest was extremely difficult. The natives kept to distinct paths or, as they preferred, traveled by canoe. There was little fear that they would be seized during their slumbers in this dense rain forest.

Five

The night was quiet and refreshing, but as dawn neared, the mist chilled the two and made them restless. The first light found them dozing fitfully. Roamer was also restless and was lurking about hoping to catch some small animal for breakfast. McDougal roused, gathered a few hanging dead limbs that were up out of the dew that dampened the ground, and rekindled the fire. Both men hunched near its meager flame, attempting to restore body warmth to a comfortable level.

"How is yer ankle this morning, M'Dougal?"

"It feels much better though it still lames me some."

The swelling had abated, but Duncan's left ankle was black and blue below the bone on the inside of the foot and all around the bone on the outside. He limbered it up, found that extremes of motion brought sharp pains, and so replaced the cloth strips he had used as bindings the day before.

"It looks as though I should use my walking stick for another day."

The discussion stopped as McTavish noticed that Roamer was no longer rummaging about but was standing still watching something down the slope. His gaze was attentive, and his throat emitted a low growl. "Ye better snuff out that fire, M'Dougal. There is something coming up the hillside following our tracks."

"I've a better thought, John. Let it draw their attention while we leave here."

"Aye," McTavish muttered in a low tone, then carefully but quickly moved down the slope to the south. McDougal followed closely behind, taking care not to leave disturbed twigs or bent ferns that would be easily followed. They crossed an open but still dark section beneath the heavy canopy of tall trees, then stopped in a thicket to watch behind. Roamer had not barked but continued to be alarmed and kept close to McTavish.

"Look, Duncan, over there."

"Yes, I see them." It was still too dark to tell how many, but several Indians could be seen moving up the hillside through the trees, moving in the direction of the adventurers' recently abandoned camp. One of the natives noticed the smoke of their warming fire and pointed it out to his companions. The Indians were apparently holding their own discussion, deciding what to do.

"What do ye make of it, Duncan? Are they following us? And if they are, why haven't they attacked the camp?"

"I don't know, but I think we should move on and with due haste. They may be coming to try to trade but that would not seem likely at this time of the morning. The Indians never come to the fort to trade until near midday. Those are probably trying to spot us. They don't want to be surprised either."

Still careful to leave no signs of their passing, the two men hastened down the hill. The bushes were still dripping with dew as they made their way in the direction McTavish had indicated. At the bank of the stream, which had now become quite small, they found a supply of salmon berries for a hasty breakfast. McDougal was also finding that his ankle had not improved as much as he had thought and was appreciating the break. Glancing down, he noted that the swelling was again appearing.

"Do ye think they are following, Duncan?"

"If they are, they are probably far behind. It hasn't been light enough to track well, and they would have first been looking in the same direction we were originally traveling—east. Our abrupt change of course may have thrown them off. What do you think?"

"I donae think they are close. Roamer seems too at ease."

"Humph, I wouldn't stake much on that dog. We better move on."

The south bank of the stream was steep, so that each man in turn slipped as he clambered up the slope. There would be no hiding the scars where leaves and fir needles had been scraped from the red clay of the hillside.

In the distance, behind the two, shouts could be heard.

"What do ye make of that, Duncan?"

"I didn't understand all of it. They were too far away."

"I do nae think a war party would make so much noise. Nor hunters. M'Dougal, what did you say to that lass yesterday?"

Duncan McDougal's ruddy face turned even redder, and he only blustered instead of answering directly. A knowing look came into McTavish's eyes.

"Aye, Duncan, I ken yer ways. 'Tis well I was along yesterday and nae off scouting the ridge, or we would be even more hotly pursued by father and brothers. We hae best be moving along smartly now."

The small stream, they found, turned and flowed from the south. For a while they rushed along deer and elk paths that paralleled the stream. The concern, now that clear tracks were left, was to travel as far and fast as they could. For the next couple of miles they followed this course until the waters of the small stream diminished and the game paths forked and spread.

Here the country opened under a canopy of tall trees. In this region, further shaded by ridges to the west and south, the moisture nourished mosses and ferns but obliged the trees and vines to reach high and spindly toward the sunlight. The result was an open, green twilight through which hung trapped remnants of the morning mist.

"How strange," commented McTavish. "It's as though the glen were enchanted and kept in a spell."

"Ah, M'Tavish, who could cast a spell on such a place?" McDougal chided.

"Who knows, perhaps a witch, hobgoblins, a warlock—it could even have been that strange fellow, Lamazee."

McDougal laughed aloud. "Come, let's change direction and cover our trail. They would least expect us to go up the slope to the west —that's the direction we were coming from."

The travelers crossed a moss and fern-carpeted valley and began to climb an open slope cut by many ravines. As they moved higher they found undergrowth, and the vine-bushes with small maple leaves were thicker, lacking in mossy coat, but heavily branched and thickly leaved. Where the leaves were exposed to spots of sunlight, they were turning crimson.

Game trails were becoming difficult to find as McDougal and Mc-Tavish turned south toward the valley of the Nehalems. They hoped that their long strides had placed them well ahead of their shorter-legged Indian pursuers. Their efforts to hide their passage would also make tracking difficult and time consuming.

Pressing on, McTavish led the way over a rise and into a ravine that led toward the bay he had seen. The ravine continued steeply for a while, then spread into a narrow valley.

McTavish stopped. "This is like the glen that I saw from the mountain, but I did nae know it was this brushy and cut up by erosion. From up there I took it to be an easy day's march."

McDougal only grunted in return while sitting on a crumbling log and considered his badly swollen ankle. "Let's stop and rest a bit. I am feeling a spell from your warlock."

"Be careful, M'Dougal, lest he place a spell on ye. Ye would look quare indeed with some of the green moss in place of yer red beard."

They both laughed for the first time since they started on their serious trip. The joking continued for a while even after Duncan rose and they resumed their trek. They decided to move higher up the slope to the west in search of more open ground. McDougal, however, was limping and obviously pained. They progressed more slowly.

As they angled higher, they traveled southerly, slowly and carefully. Suddenly McTavish, who was still in the lead, stopped and studied the ground. He looked to the right, then to the left, and turned to face his companion.

"Duncan, this appears to be a trail. It is too straight and distinct for an elk path—it must be an Indian trail."

McDougal pulled himself forward to view the discovery. "I agree, John, but it doesn't look like it has been used recently."

"No, it does nae. I see no tracks, and the leaves of the plants hae nae been disturbed."

"Well, it goes in the direction we want, and it would be easier walking. Let's follow it for a while."

So it was that the travelers stumbled upon the trail that passed to the east of the Neahkanie peaks. They found the going much easier through the balance of the morning, though they were constantly wary lest the pursuers catch up with them.

As midday approached, the hungry, weary men broke out into an open space in which scattered alder trees and bushes grew. From this location they could look down and ahead and see a broad valley with winding streams before them.

Berries were abundant in the bushes so the two stopped to eat. John had laid aside his rifle and wandered a few feet farther along the trail, gathering in the sweet, juicy blackberries of the vines along the path. McDougal stayed behind, gathering fruit from a huckleberry bush beneath the trail. Roamer wandered in the hillside above, searching for squirrels or mice.

Suddenly a small bear burst from the slope above, tumbled onto the trail, and ran almost straight for McDougal. There was little time to react, but Duncan swept around instinctively with his walking shaft. This was an opportunity for a meal of fresh meat.

Duncan intended to strike a blow on the head of the animal. In its swift but clumsy passage, however, his blow went amiss and struck the creature on the back, temporarily paralyzing its hind legs. Emitting a pig-like squeal, it dragged its malfunctioning back legs and left a trail of urine as it struggled to leave the path. McDougal stepped forward to deal a final blow when his attention was abruptly drawn elsewhere.

Above the trail ahead of him, a fearsome roar sounded, followed by the noise of bushes being crushed asunder. A huge black bear was responding to the wails of her injured offspring and was destroying anything in her path.

The black fury swept onto the trail at the spot where John McTavish was interrupted in his berry-gathering. With one bounding stride, John cleared the path, leaped for the limbs of an alder tree and swung up into its shelter as the bear roared past. Duncan looked into a dark face, its eyes reduced by hatred to mere slits. Below the eyes, snarling lips dripped saliva and berry juice, curling away to show monstrous fanged teeth. He was rooted, hardly realizing that his staff had been swept from his hand by a swift, swiping blow of a sharp-nailed paw.

Suddenly the savage face disappeared into a whirl of black-furred bulk. The bear was striking at something at its heels. Duncan caught a glimpse of brown as a smaller animal darted to the side. Roamer was nipping at the bear's heels.

For a few brief moments the bear stood on three legs, growling and occasionally striking a raised paw at the quickly darting dog. Then the huge animal followed its cub down the slope into the valley below, stopping at times to look back and snarl a warning to potential followers.

Sheepisly McTavish climbed down from the tree. "Aye, Duncan, that was close. Are ye hurt? I am a wee bit ashamed to hae wandered from my rifle."

"No. No, the bear didn't harm me, though I seem to have lost my walking stick.

"I'll not be eating your dog, though. He has earned a place along the trail. And I didn't think he even liked me."

"Aye, he's not a bad dog, are ye, Roamer? Here, you hae earned a bit of jerky."

"Yes, he has. Let's see if he will take some of mine, too."

For a few moments Roamer enjoyed the attention of both men. The possibility of pursuit had been forgotten during the incident. The barking of a squirrel on the ridge they had recently crossed brought the possibility back to them.

"Aye, tha' was close, M'Dougal, but I think we should start on. I am nae convinced we are nae still being followed."

"That could be. I wonder, though, why no one seems to have passed on this trail—and why these berries have not been gathered. They are going past their prime."

"Aye, perhaps it is some sort of a spell."

Duncan shook his head as he reached for a stout vine maple limb from which to fashion a new walking stick. He didn't believe in spells, but he didn't think this was the time to debate the matter. He was more concerned about what was disturbing the squirrel on the hillside. It could be a fox, or it could be the Nehaynehums.

John McTavish and Duncan McDougal hurried on. The trail continued to be empty except for their passing. An hour passed and there was no sign of pursuit. The pace slackened, and they became more relaxed. Within the next hour they were glimpsing the marsh at the upper end of the estuary as they passed breaks between the trees along the trail. Flocks of waterfowl would occasionally rise up and fly along the river. But there was no evidence of the Nehalems: no lodges, no berry pickers, no fishermen—nothing to confirm the existence of an Indian settlement.

"Do you think this could be the wrong river?"

"I would nae think so. It is the first possible water course south of the Neahkanie peaks. It looks ideal for settlement. Look at the abundance of birds in the marshes, and the stream is plenty large enough for salmon. It does nae make sense, mon."

McDougal pointed out across the valley to the east. "There is even another stream flowing out of the valley, or perhaps another fork of the stream below us. Combined they provide enough water to pass a fair sized ship.

"If this isn't the valley of the Nehalems, it should be peopled with another group."

Slowly and cautiously they followed the trail, past the joining of the two streams, past low islands, around a point of land to a wide marsh cut with several channels. Beyond the marsh were the quiet waters of a large bay.

"This must be the body of water tha' I saw from the mountain. Yon sand dunes is the strip of land that separates the bay from the ocean."

"John, I don't feel we should follow this trail much farther. It crosses too much open ground—too far from cover, yet too close to the trees if someone has a mind to waylay us."

"We can climb this little hill and look on to where we are going. Now, Duncan, do you feel the spell on this place?"

"Yes," McDougal replied, "I am beginning to." He was serious.

They did not hesitate to climb the hill to look over the country ahead. Both men were as anxious as they had been on the first night's march. Something was very wrong, for this peaceful valley, a paradise, should have been filled with happy voices. Instead, its paths were empty and unused, its fruits ignored, and its hunting grounds untouched. There was something foreboding about the quiet.

Carefully the two worked their way onto the little wooded knoll. Duncan cast aside his staff, feeling that it hindered his crawling up the slope noiselessly and, in a confrontation, might be interpreted as a sign of weakness.

The brush was fairly dense and devoid of game trails, but they were able to reach the crest without making much noise. Unlike the rocky mountain that McTavish found near the end of their first day of travel, this knoll was covered with trees. They searched for an opening that would give them a clear view of the valley but were obliged to continue over onto the western slope before finding even a small clearing.

Through the opening in the trees, a panorama lay before the men. The wide flow of the river wound around the marshy flats and looped to the northwest. There it met the long line of sand dunes and was diverted southward. The river mouth was not visible beyond the forested points of land that reached down to the waters of the bay. Straight ahead of the travelers, before a line of sand dunes that shielded them from the sea, rose a number of Indian lodges.

"Well, John, this seems to be the village of the Nehalems."

"Aye, but I do nae see anybody aboot."

As the late afternoon shadows lengthened, the men lay in the cover of the trees on the hillside and watched. A few Nehalems appeared briefly, but there seemed to be little activity.

"Wha' do ye make of it, M'Dougal?"

"I don't know. It isn't natural. There should be more going on."

"Are they fishing—or gone raiding?"

"I don't think so. Their large canoes for travel at sea are on the bank, and these people don't like to walk far."

"Do ye think we should stay here for the night?"

"No, I don't think so. If a raiding party is gone they may return tomorrow. We would also stand a better chance of escape if night were close at hand. I think we should go to the village now and find out what we came here to learn."

"Are ye well enough in yer leg, Duncan?"

"It is well enough to run on if I have to."

Still they did not move. They continued to observe for another quarter of an hour before beginning to descend the lookout hill. The descent was slow. McTavish noticed the difficulty McDougal was having with his swollen ankle and asked, "Are ye sure ye do nae want me to fetch ye a shaft?"

"No, I would run better without it. I will stop favoring my leg as soon as we get in sight of the village. We mustn't show any sign of weakness. Do you remember our troubles up the Columbia River? Any time the Indians knew a party to have sickness or injury they were sure to take advantage of it to do their mischief."

"Aye, I remember quite well at the rapids."

When the two broke out onto the open plain, they walked upright and nonchalantly toward the village, cradling their rifles in their arms but showing no alarm. As they approached the first lodge, an old woman scuttled by in front of them with an armload of firewood, ignoring them. Not so the village dogs, who came forward barking noisily and sniffing at Roamer. They were a poor-looking band of mongrels, gaunt and unwilling to do more than voice a challenge to the strangers and their dog.

Several of the lodges they passed looked empty. No smoke came from the roofs although this was the time of day when Indians would normally be preparing meals. A few children appeared in the doorway of the next lodge, but no crowd gathered. In fact, the Nehalems seemed to be paying them little heed.

McTavish was fighting an irresistable urge to turn and look behind when he noticed an older man standing in the doorway of a lodge, watching the arrival of the white men. He had the bearing of a chief, but his expression gave no clues to his disposition or intentions.

"Wha' do ye make of it, Duncan?"

"I don't know, but perhaps we can deal with this fellow. Let's smile and walk right up to him like we know what we are about."

"Perhaps we should ask for Lamazee. He could help us if he would. At least they might think we had come to visit him."

McDougal led the way straight toward the man, who stood waiting. As they approached, the Nehalem raised his hand in a peaceful gesture. McDougal raised his hand in a similar gesture and spoke. "Hello. Is Lamazee here?" He paused, then repeated—"Lamazee?"

"Hello," responded the Nehalem. "Lamazee not here."

McTavish and McDougal looked at each other in astonishment. After a hesitation Duncan cautiously asked, "Do you speak English?"

"I speak the bearded ones' tongue to some length."

The traders were too surprised to respond. McTavish drew up beside McDougal, but still did not speak. It was the Nehalem who broke the silence.

"I learn from men who come in big canoe with sails—goes with the wind," the Indian volunteered, making a gesture to symbolize a ship sailing out on the bay. "I am Yakala. Lamazee is not here; he is gone away."

The statement was puzzling. McDougal and McTavish did not know whether Lamazee was merely off on a trading or fishing trip, or if he might have been expelled from the tribe. Yakala's expression did not reveal his meaning, but McDougal guessed it may have been the latter and that he had better not express friendship with Lamazee.

"Oh, that is alright. We came here to talk and knew that Lamazee could interpret for us. But he is not needed—obviously—and we would prefer to talk directly with you.

"I am Duncan McDougal; this man is John McTavish. We are partners with the North West Fur Company and come to seek trade with your people. Last year your people came to trade with us, but they have not come this year. We hope we have not offended you. We have tried to trade fairly with the Nehalems and wonder why your people have not returned."

"Ya hase—look," Yakala said, sadness entering his voice. He waved his arm in the direction of the lodges the white men had passed. "My people are beset by evil spirits. They are very sick. Many have gone to Memaloose Illahee—the land of the dead. Even Loatle, the medicine man, has died, and his spirit has left us."

John and Duncan turned and looked toward the nearest lodge. Through the open doorway they could see a woman moving about within the blue veil of smoke from the cooking fire. Near the doorway lay a child apparently asleep in a pile of furs.

The woman turned, silhouetted against the glow of the fire, then shuffled toward the child. She placed a hand on the youngster's forehead, then drawing back a fur robe, took the child's shoulders. As she lifted gently, the small head fell back limply. Holding the small body closer, the woman placed her head to the child's chest. Gently she lay the small form back down and kneeled beside the pile of furs.

Wails of "Ah-ee, ah-ee" drifted from the blue darkness of the lodge.

"Come," signalled Yakala, sadness welling in his voice, "let us walk over the dunes to the sea. It is well to move ourselves from the calls of death and to smell the wind that blows over the waves."

The three men threaded their way past silent lodges, piles of discards, and sullen dogs.

"Aye, Duncan, they are beset by smallpox. That child over there bears the red marks."

"Yes, but the Clatsops and Killamuks have suffered smallpox before. I've seen scars when they came to visit. It should not be affecting them this much."

"The evil spirits you call 'small pox'—they come again," interjected Yakala. "It is the doing of Lamazee."

"Aye, this Lamazee must be an evil one. Tell me, Yakala, where did this Lamazee come from? He does nae look like one of your people."

"He came with the sail canoe many, many summers ago. He was then yet a child, the slave of one of their types."

"Did ye know him well?"

"I knew him since he came to the Nehalems, but there is much to be known of Lamazee, and I do not know—do not understand—all there is."

"Would ye tell us aboot him?"

"Yes, but let us walk closer to the sea. It is best not to speak of him in the village."

As they walked along, Yakala noticed Roamer and seemed to be appraising him. McTavish watched with a spark of pride in the dog that was now one of the group.

"You have nice dog," Yakala spoke at last. "He is good. We have only the thin ones left. Your dog is well filled out—would make good meal. The night has fallen many times since there was good food in the Nehalem bellies. Perhaps with a full belly the Nehalem men would go and take the salmon. Then things would be better."

McTavish turned to McDougal but didn't speak. Neither man wanted to deny the tribe that which might bring them the will to survive, but they didn't want to part with Roamer. Certainly not as a meal. McTavish felt his mouth turn dry.

Six

"We sit here on the sand dunes," spoke Yakala, "and look at the ocean from which it all began—the coming of the bear-people and the end of the Nehalems. It was from out there," he said, gesturing, "that the evil sail canoe came to enter our waters, the Nehalem. Since that day I have seen much of its evil ways and learned more from Lamazee's stories."

"Wha' did the sailing ship look like?" McTavish asked. He had dreamed of a ship.

"The great wings—the sails—were the color of the sand that is darkened by the ocean's waves, but the body of the sail canoe and all other things about it were black—black as the raven that dwells in the dark forest."

John was astonished by the description, which seemed to correspond with what he had seen in his dream. He listened intently as Yakala, his brown, leathery face wrinkled in anguish, related the tale of the wind canoe.

The ship had been coasting slowly northward, moving carefully around the headlands and following the lines of beaches. It had almost passed the Nehalem entrance when it turned toward the shore. The tide was high, and no breakers could be seen in the channel. For a while the ship hesitated outside of the entrance, as though to survey the river mouth and the quiet bay within, then the great wings were spread and the ship slipped into the bay.

For the first two days the ship lay at anchor around a point to the south but within sight of the Nehalem village. The Indians did not venture to greet the dark vessel, and the ship's company kept busy with chores. Yakala felt that repairs were being made after a long journey, for the sailors climbed all over the tall trees that held the wings and chopped new parts from the nearby forest.

The Nehalems watched but were wary of the strangers with hairy faces. Some thought the newcomers to be a strange form of bears, but all were awed by the immenseness of their war canoe and the mysterious war-clubs the bear-men carried. These clubs were strong medicine, for the bear people merely pointed them at game, and thunder would strike the creatures down. During this time the Nehalems saw nothing of Jack Ramsay, for he had been doing his best to stay out of sight of the crew members and was scurrying around like the bilge-rats that inhabited the ship's dark corners.

Eventually the Nehalems became more bold. In time, their curiosity took them to the ship. Jack was drawn by the sounds of the visit, and they had seen the red-haired Lamazee for the first time, peering over the rail at the canoes. The confrontation had brought an immediate reaction from the Nehalems. He lacked the facial hair of the bear-people—he was beardless like they were. Also, since they had never seen red hair before, Jack's flaming red hair was somehow supernatural. The Nehalems were attracted to him and tried to converse with him while still distrusting the large, hairy crewmen.

To one of the maidens, Lemolo, Jack Ramsay was particularly important. She was born a slave but had successfully avoided becoming the possession of any of the Nehalem men by telling the story that Talapus would send a young god from the sea to marry her. The story had been losing its power, but Lemolo realized Jack Ramsay could make it live.

The Nehalems, who possessed slaves, were quick to note the status of Ramsay as indentured like a slave. This undermined Lemolo's claim, and opinions were split among the superstitious Nehalems. On the other hand, it was apparent to the white men that Ramsay was given special regard by the Indians, and they used this. His status, at least as far as the Indians were concerned, changed—to Lemolo's benefit.

"Well, Mr. Smythe," said Captain Beasely one evening, "you seem to have a real jewel there. With a little encouragement your lad should be able to talk the very teeth out of these aborigines."

"You mean the way they gathered around Ramsay. Yes, I was thinking of that. There must be some way we can use their ignorance."

"Why not elevate him to the post of clerk? At least while we are here, he could strut around and attract their attention while we deal them out of their goods. Did you see the furs some of them were wearing? Why not get your new clerk to do some trading for us?"

"Yes, captain, I think you are right. If one of your men can find the wretch and bring him here, we will start his instruction."

"Ah, Mr. Smythe, remember that he is to be a clerk. We must treat him with some respect, at least while there is trading to be done."

After a time Jack was brought, cowering and expecting the lash, before trader Smythe and Captain Beasely. He was confused when he was accorded the unexpected treatment of being seated in a chair. As soon as he had calmed enough that he would not bolt out of the cabin, he was released by the seamen who had brought him.

Smythe was the first to speak. "Now, lad, let's see, your given name is Jack, isn't it? Well, you have been a good servant on the trip, and we have decided to reward you with a promotion to clerk."

Ramsay sat silently, not knowing what this meant. He had come to know this entire group as an abusive bunch of ruffians. Not one had come forward to befriend him, and he had been the object of derision by all.

"You seem to have a good head on your shoulders, Jack," Captain Beasely interjected, "so we have decided to see what you can do as one of our traders."

"Thank you, sir-r," the boy managed after a long pause.

Captain Beasely rummaged through a chest for a few moments and extracted a shirt and trousers. Some additional pawing in the depths of the sea chest brought out a pair of stockings with holes in them.

"You will have to be clean and dress appropriately. Fetch a bucket of water to the deck and wash, then put these clothes on. They will take a bit of cutting down and mending, but they will do for now. And stay out of the scummy bilges."

"We will need to get him a pair of shoes, Captain. I may have an old pair that will fit him reasonably well.

"Go clean up now, Jack, and come back so we can tell you what to do."

Jack approached the cabin door with trepidation. He knew that some of the crew would be lingering outside. What he didn't know was that the two who had brought him to Captain Beasely's cabin had hung around eavesdropping, hoping for the fun of watching a flogging. They were now off spreading the work of their surprising discovery. The whole ship's company was quickly aware of Jack's sudden worth.

To Jack's surprise he received a lot of stares and furtive looks from the crew but no harrassment. Even when he brought the bucket of water to a corner of the deck, scrubbed himself, and put on the ridiculously large clothes, no one uttered a word of contempt. He was still walking lightly as he carried the empty bucket back to its rack, and as he came below, he overheard the discussion of two of the men. "It *is* weird, isn't it, the way these savages have taken a likin' to the boy."

"Aye, ev'ry time they look at him, it is as though someone casts a spell over them. They are a dumb lot, to be sure."

"Well, if I know the conniving of Jacob Smythe and our captain, we should be able to count on this to keep the blighters from cuttin' our throats in the night."

"Much more than that, Ben. Haven't you heard? They are going to use the lad in the trading. While he is keeping them entranced, we can cheat them out of their very skins, let alone all of the beavers and otters they can catch."

The laughter of the two men covered the sound of Jack's foot-falls as he placed the bucket in the rack and departed. Now he knew the reason for his "promotion," but it didn't matter. He was too desperate to care, and the Indians were no friends of his either. He knew he was being ill-used, but perhaps he would get a chance to turn this to his own advantage.

Jack knocked timidly at the door to the captain's cabin.

"Come in, lad. Let's have a look at you."

Smythe startled Jack by seizing him by the back of the shirt, but the fear was only momentary. "The shirt needs some taking in here. I think you can cut out this much and sew it back together—or maybe just sew a seam down here to hold it.

"It will do for starts, and I will give you another shirt from the trade goods. Also some pants. The ones you have on will do if you cut some off the legs."

Captain Beasely handed Jack some scissors and a threaded needle. "You can work on your clothes while you listen to instruction on your new duties."

As Jack worked on his garments, he learned that he was to acquire as much of the native language as he could so that he might translate Smythe's offers and encourage the natives to accept them. He would make friends and gain the confidence of the Indians and try to learn where other groups with furs to trade might live. Jack was clumsy in his sewing, and the shirt was bunched in back, but the appearance in front was satisfactory to the captain and his employer. They dismissed him.

For the first time in many months, Jack was able to sleep out on deck, although he was fearful of wandering far from the protection of the captain's and trader's cabins. He was already beginning to like his new status.

On the following morning Jack was decked out in his new finery, and the trading efforts began. There were many sly sneers from the crewmen, but these were such an improvement over the overt hazing that Jack didn't mind. He was also given his first opportunity to set foot on the shore since he had been dragged aboard the dark ship.

This first acquaintance with the Nehalems was not very profitable. It had never occurred to the Nehalems that they should hunt and stockpile beaver and otter pelts. Thus it took a while for Smythe to indicate through gestures that furs, like the few fur ornaments, were what he wanted. While the fur robes brought from the lodges were frequently old and worn, the few fresh ones were purchased with bright cloth and trinkets. Hopefully the Indians would seek out more fresh furs to trade

To Jack this first encounter was bewildering and the relationship distant. He was unaccustomed to his new clothes and his new status. Also, he was surrounded by wild people speaking a strange tongue, about what he knew not but could only fear. Their garb was skimpy and different, and their foreheads were strangely flattened, giving their eyes a wild protruding appearance. He stood back, silent and shy, while the trading was going on. This didn't help his god-like image with the Nehalems, but at the same time Jack seemed less like a slave. At first the Indians looked at him in awe, then some came close enough to touch him and feel the garments he wore. As time passed, they became more bold. Then their interest diminished—everyone's except Lemolo's. She sat entranced, watching Jack and hoping for a sign. Jack did notice her, but the only feeling he showed was embarrassment. Her head had not been distorted, but she and the other slaves with normal facial features were not permitted to come forward to trade.

When their interest in Jack diminished, so did the trading prospects. At first Smythe was able to obtain fur robes for trivial trinkets, but as attention waned, many of the Indians wandered off. Those who remained became more astute in their trading, gesturing that they wanted knives like one of the crew had produced to cut the rawhide thongs from decorative pelts Smythe had purchased.

As they rowed back to the ship, which was anchored across the channel from the village (far enough not to be surprised by canoe-loads of warriors), Smythe made his observation known to the new assistant.

"Jack, my lad, you've got to take more interest in your endeavors if you have a mind to keep your promotion. I want you to get involved in the trading. Next time we go ashore, you are to help in the bartering, and you must start to learn their language. Make an effort to learn their words for the things we want to obtain and the objects we are giving in return. I want you to memorize the words, and I want you to tell me what you have learned. Did you learn any of their words to-day?"

"No—no, sir."

"Well, pay a mind to it next time. If you don't—well, if you aren't a value to us in trading, you will have to go back to the chores you were doing before. And you won't like that."

"Yes, sir-r."

The threat was obvious, and it sent a chill along Jack's spine. Above all, he didn't want to return to the miserable state he had endured before. He would prefer to run away and take his chances with the Indians rather than suffer that again. Though it was apparent that Lemolo and others were held as chattel, Jack's impression was that the Nehalems treated their slaves better than he had been treated.

Jack had been elated with the improvement of his lot. Now he felt a weakening of his position. The only sounds in the longboat were the squeak of the oar-locks and the swish of the oars. By the time they reached the side of the ship, Jack had resolved to perform his new tasks diligently, but if the threat to return him to his previous despair was carried out, he would escape to this wilderness land and its strange people.

During the next two weeks trading improved. Indians were gather-ing otters and beavers from their familiar coves and streams and bringing the fresh pelts to trade. These had to be salted down and dried, but most were in prime condition. Jack was learning his trade well, personally trading for most of the better elaka, the Indian name for the sea otter. Exchange was in trinkets, but he learned that the villagers preferred knives and hatchets. His compulsion to learn their language impressed the Indians, though he was unable to properly pronounce many of the words. Some were disdainful of his inability, but others regarded his speech with awe, allowing it to feed their mystical assumptions about him.

Things were going well. The Nehalems were obtaining hatchets that cut firewood with ease and knives that greatly reduced the difficulty of skinning and cutting up game. The men obtained pretty baubles to attract the women they desired. All of these things were to be had in exchange for the otters and beavers that were so plentiful. And Jack was learning his lessons well.

But, things changed. Baubles and beads were no longer new. It took more of them to impress an Indian and to gain his furs. Similarly the second knife or hatchet that a primitive man sees is not as desirable as the first. The traders wanted to pay the same amounts while the otters were becoming harder to find. Exchanges became difficult.

During the trading, Lemolo had found many excuses to wander by. She could not participate in the discussions, but she annointed herself with salmon oil as was the custom of native finery and walked by as slowly and closely as she dared. The red-headed youth seemed unimpressed. Lemolo tried a little more scented oil and came even closer. The reaction was the opposite from what she had hoped. It was obvious that the bear people were unaccustomed to the use of native perfumes. Although she could not have understood the words, "Whew, that stinks," she must have gathered the meaning from the accompanying gestures and tone of voice.

Lemolo hurriedly bathed in the river, washing away all of the precious salmon oil, and tried again. The results were elating. She was rewarded by a smiling look of approval from Jack. This was progress.

By the time trading was declining, near the end of the second week, Lemolo was the recipient of many glances from the red-headed god of her dreams. Her mind was awhirl with the sensations of young love. Jack's companions were saying things to him that caused him to blush at times and look up at her. He also directed occasional words at her, words she didn't understand but which had softness to them. If only the red-headed one would give presents to her father, the master of her slave-wife mother, and seek to make Lemolo his woman.

Seven

Fair skies along the northwest coast normally bring afternoon winds from the north. With the winds come choppy seas that bounce a small ship badly, but the breeze is dependable. From the time it arises, generally by noon, until it abates at sunset, it can be relied upon by captains of sailing ships to provide continuous power for their vessels.

One morning the bear people did not come ashore. Instead, they were seen moving their ship, climbing upon the tall trees the craft carried, and making preparations with the big, gray cloths that were tied to the main limbs close to the base of the trees. Each tree had one low-lying big limb on which rested such a cloth. There was a second limb on each tree, much higher than the lower one, and smaller. And sometimes, a third, smaller cloth hung above that.

Lemolo sat upon the dunes. She had bathed in the river that morning and carefully smoothed her hair. A new skirt of reeds was tied about her waist, but otherwise she had turned her brown skin to the warmth of the sun. She watched and waited for the bear people and the red-haired man-god.

Suddenly she stood up. The big cloths were spreading up the tall trees like the wings of an enormous bird. What could this mean?

To her dismay, some of the bear people were moving around in a circle chanting a strange melody. An object came up out of the water, and the sail canoe began to move. Men high in the trees were spreading some of the smaller cloths and strange slanting sheets of gray were moving upward in the front of the canoe. Westward the ship moved, toward the bend in the wide river; then, as the great wings swung to one side, it turned south along the channel and away from her.

Lemolo ran to the water's edge, but the ship was rapidly moving away, heading for the mouth of the bay. She looked wildly for Jack, but the people in the ship were now mere specks, and she could not discern him.

Breathlessly, she ran across the dunes to the beach. As she reached the sands before the breakers, she stopped and looked to the south. The ship was just passing through the swells at the bar and was slipping out to sea. Twice the ship lurched as waves struck the bow, sending spray cascading down on the forward deck. Then it moved silently out into the open ocean.

The ship heeled over on a larboard tack and headed out to the northwest. Winds were picking up enough that the ship was far out to sea in a short time, taking her red-headed god with it. Could he have been standing at the rail looking back at her? She couldn't tell, for the mouth of the river was almost four miles from where she stood on the beach, across the dunes from the village. Lemolo watched as the ship became smaller in the distance, then her heart beat faster as she saw it turn toward the shore to the north of where she stood. Perhaps it was coming back. But, though the ship was turned in an angle toward shore, it still moved northward. Then, as suddenly as it had turned before, it turned away to the northwest again and soon was lost from view beyond the western reaches of Neahkanie Mountain.

What Lemolo could not have known was that the traders had become restless. Since she and the other slaves did not participate in the trading she had not known that the flow of valuable pelts had been tapering off, and that the Nehalems had been demanding more and more trade goods for each fur. The spells of Lamazee, as Jack Ramsay called himself with his impaired speech, and as the Indians came to call him, had weakened on the Nehalems. The traders were going elsewhere to seek their fortune.

The winds of the north brought fair skies and reliable winds to the mariners, but to Jack Ramsay the accompanying waves brought a renewal of the stomach problems he had encountered on his first days at sea. Adding to his troubles was the fact that, out of sight of the Indians, he was no longer useful in trading and so was given many of his old chores. Nor was the crew restrained any longer. Though they were not as wont to abuse him physically, the harsh heckling returned. Life was almost as bad as before. If he didn't get out of the way of a crewman fast enough he could expect a swift kick or a cuff on the ear. There were also many jokes about his sudden trips to the rail to relieve his stricken stomach.

Jack's master, while not making any effort to restrain the crew, did not add particularly to his misery. Outside of the usual chores, he made no great demands on the boy. Smythe knew that if the boy's red hair and hairless face had entranced one group of Indians it might well give him a trading advantage with others.

During the weeks with the Nehalems, Jack had gained a new strength from his improved lot. He was developing the seeds of a resolve not to return to his earlier depths. Perhaps he was growing —and perhaps he would find a way to strike back at his tormentors.

With nightfall the winds and waves abated and so did the evils of seasickness. The next two days brought afternoon gales and heavy swells, but they were better than the first for Jack as the nausea did not return. The wind and seas also kept the men busy enough that they did not find as much time to harrass the boy.

On the fourth day the captain noted a large inlet and headed the ship to the east. They passed a wild and rocky headland and moved into an inland sea. In these quieter waters they sought villages with which to pursue their business. The first one lacked a harbor suitable for the ship so Jack and his master, with a crew to row, were sent out in the longboat.

The group wasn't far from the ship when the noticed several canoes slipping into the water. Rowing slowed as the crafts came closer. Suddenly a shower of arrows rained around and into the longboat, though miraculously no one was injured. The crew stopped rowing, crouched behind the gunwale, and fired at the Indians with their rifles. Several of the natives, standing to discharge arrows, were hit and tumbled into the water with loud cries. As swiftly as they had come, the canoes departed. The longboat returned to the ship unharmed, but with no profit for the day.

At the next village they again found no harbor and were forced to use the longboat. This time the men were better armed, and a cannon was prepared on the ship to support them if needed. As they cautiously approached, Jack was made to stand upright in the bow, where the Indians could see his red hair. Either this tactic was successful or Indians of this village were less aggressive. No weapons were visible in the hands of the villagers as the longboat moved carefully up to the beach.

Unlike the Nehalems, this group of Indians had seen white men before and had previously traded furs. It had been months since another trading vessel had called, so trade pelts were stored in the longhouse.

This people was a tribe called Quiliutes or Kwilihutes, and they spoke a language with some similarities to the Nehalem tongue. Ramsay had learned his previous lessons well and, prodded by his recent partial loss of status and threats of total misery, immediately became involved in trading. He made a serious effort to learn the key words of this language and used them at every opportunity. Unlike the other traders who continued to impose English words upon the savages, Ramsay was trying hard to use the tongue of his newfound acquaintances. To his delight the Indians did not appear to mind the manner in which he pronounced their words, did not laugh or otherwise suffer him any indignity for errors in pronunciation. They soon turned to him for their trading and he to the Indians for limited conversations.

The ship stayed in the area for about three weeks, trading with the various groups that had furs to exchange or were able to gather fresh pelts. Although Lamazee found no close friends among the Quiliutes, he learned to communicate well and was at ease in their villages. Their communities, in fact, were to be preferred to the insecurities of the ship.

By the third week, fur supplies in the area were dwindling, and the natives with the greatest abilities for acquiring pelts had received about all the trade goods they desired. The anchor was weighed, and the ship moved deeper into the inland sea looking for other peoples to trade with. None were found, so the course was set back to the open sea and northward.

The land they followed showed other indentations though none of the others were as large as the passage into the inland sea. The inlets were peopled, however, and most had furs to be exchanged. Jack found some similarities of language between the northern groups and the Quiliutes. He was quickly picking up the differences and applying his knowledge well.

The next large sound was the home of a tribe called the Clayoquots. It was a large sound with many inlets and an abundance of sea otters. Two other ships, the brig *HANCOCK* and the ship *GRACE*, were already trading in the sound. They were American ships, and their captains, Crowell and Coolidge, were not inclined to pry into the affairs of the dark ship. Thus, they were no threat.

However, the natives were aloof and accustomed to fair prices for their pelts. They approached the strange ship with "Waa'com," which means friendship, but had little they wished to trade. Furthermore, they appeared unimpressed with Jack and preferred to deal directly with Jacob Smythe. They had been quick to perceive that it was he, not Jack, who was the trading authority. Jack's pride smarted from this, for he was being rebuffed in the one area where he had gained status. The Clayoquots did not offer friendship to Jack, and he nurtured a hatred for the Clayoquots.

Although the American captains had not pried into the affairs of the traders in the dark ship and had kept their distance, Captain Beasely was uneasy. In addition, an English ship might appear in so popular a location. The natives were too independent for the furs to be obtained at a low price. All they had to do was wait for the next ship to come around and try for a better deal.

The uneasiness increased until, without warning, Captain Beasely ordered the anchor weighed and the sails hoisted. Since a fair and constant wind was blowing, the captain chose to coast along close to the north shore. Suddenly, as they rounded a point, they were confronted by another ship. It was British, with a large Union Jack fluttering in the breeze and a long row of gun ports. To the dismay of Captain Beasely, the newcomer was standing rapidly in from the sea and was outboard of his course. They were trapped between the British ship and the rocks, with no room to maneuver.

"God, sir," Symington sputtered, "look at those gun ports! What is she? Is she goin' to take us?"

"I don't know. She is just a sloop, but she could be a King's cutter or the tender for a man-of-war coming in just behind her."

"She doesn't seem to be goin' to take us on 'er own. I don't hear them beatin' to quarters, and they 'aven't opened the gun ports yet."

The two vessels were broadside, about to meet and pass, as Captain Beasely put his telescope to the newcomer, then burst into a frenzy of laughter.

"What? What is it, Captain?"

"Here, look her over yourself, Symington. That is just the trading sloop *JACKALL*. Most of those gun ports are painted on.

"But she could just as well have been a man-of-war. Bring us around to port and away from these points so that we have no more surprises."

The unnerving encounter with the *JACKALL* brought back the concerns that had motivated Captain Beasely to have the hull scraped after the near-capture by the man-of-war. That evening he picked a secluded cove that was uninhabited but provided a shallow, gravelly beach. Early the following morning he had the ship brought into shallow water and lines run to trees on shore. Everything on deck was lashed down, and as the extremely low tide of the morning left the ship high out of the water, she was careened so the port side was up. All hands turned out to scrape the side. Long garlands of seaweed hung dripping beneath the bottom of the hull. A layer of moss-like algae and barnacles covered everything below the water line.

The men worked feverishly to bare the planking. Then, as the surface of the wood was drying, crew members brought driftwood from the beach and started a fire near the ship. They placed a kettle of pitch on the fire, and as soon as the side of the hull looked ready to Captain Beasely, the men began to paint the planking with hot pitch.

While the captain supervised the painting, Symington carefully worked his way along ahead of the painters, inspecting the hull for teredo damage and weakening seams. He had been satisfied with what he had seen so far. There were some teredo holes, but they were still small, and the hot pitch would kill the animals. Near the bow he stopped and scowled. "Bloar! Fetch the caulking irons and hammers! And a bundle of oakum."

"What is it, Symington?" asked the captain.

"We have lost a little caulking, not much. But we had better fill it in while we have the opportunity."

Symington and Bloar hurridly tamped lengths of oakum into the gaps between the planks as the rest of the crew painted toward them. By the time the tide returned, the crew had succeded in graving the port side.

The men were standing in water to their knees by the time the job was finished. They did not mind, however, as the water flowing into the cove crossed stones that had been warmed by the sun. The fire was out, the pitch pot and caulking irons had been handed aboard, and they could relax. One of the men stretched out in the warm water and swam a short distance from the ship. Another joined him, then still another.

It was a rare peaceful moment. Beyond the swimmers were the blue waters of the Pacific Ocean, gently pulsing from the swells that rolled in from beyond the men's imaginations. Toward the shore, the ship was slowly righting itself like a stretching giant. The dark rigging stood silhouetted against a cloudless blue sky.

Jack was not with the men in the water. He stood at the rail, silently looking down at them.

"Hugh, look at Ramsay there at the gun'l. I swear he is getting stranger every day."

"Don't you worry none, Andrew. He may be thinking mean things but he ain't big enough to carry them out."

They looked up again and Jack was gone.

The afternoon tide was not low enough to careen the starboard side. They were obliged to stay in the cove another day so they spent the time refilling water casks and gathering wood for the cookstove in the galley.

With the low tide of the following morning, they careened the ship again and graved the starboard side. There was not time for relaxing swims this day, however. As they were finishing, a canoe of Indians came by, but, after looking them over, turned and left without a word.

"Hurry, lads, I don't like the looks of that," Captain Beasely shouted. "Get the equipment aboard and the lines loosed from the trees. I want her ready to be pulled out with the anchor as soon as there is enough water."

His orders were quickly carried out. They had only to wait for the incoming tide which was very slow in returning that morning. As they waited, the canoe returned with two others full of natives, but they didn't approach.

"Get the boarding nets up. Issue each man two muskets and a cutlass. If only they hold off a little more we can break out the cannon." The ship had two cannon on carriages, but they were usually hidden under canvas and ropes near the forward mast. With the ship on her side, the crew could neither roll them into position nor depress their muzzles sufficiently to fire at the canoes.

More canoes arrived, and they began to close on the hapless ship. "Cavendish, Bloar, Arnold, fire your muskets at them!"

They did, but the distance was beyond range. Musket balls dropped harmlessly between the canoes. It was enough of a show of force, however, to show the Indians the men in the ship would fight, and they stopped paddling. For a few moments the warriors in the canoes conferred. Then, several of the dugouts turned to shore. Men with bows and arrows, and a few muskets, stepped ashore and disappeared into the trees. A trickle of water had passed beneath the ship. The tide was reaching across the beach.

More canoes arrived. As the warriors proceeded through the trees along the shore, the canoes encircled the mouth of the cove. They were in position to attack. An arrow thumped to the deck near Jack. He stared at it, a long shaft with a wicked-looking tip of bone carved so it had two barbs as well as a point. He wondered what these people would do with him. They had not received him with friendship; the savages would probably kill him along with the crew and trader Smythe. If only this were happening with the Nehalems. Jack was sure that he could learn to live with them and that with Lemolo's help he would be accepted.

The water stretching toward shore was still only a few inches deep as the ring began to close. The warriors in the trees were too far away to be accurate with their fire, but they could harrass the crew while the men from the canoes swarmed aboard.

Suddenly there was a shout, and the canoes abruptly turned and the warriors paddled to shore. The Indians in the canoes crouched low, as near to sheltering limbs as possible, and peered out to sea. Soon a sail was seen in the distance. A ship was passing.

"If only we could work a cannon," muttered Symington, "we could fire a signal."

But they couldn't. The ship was too far out in the strait to see a ship so dark that it blended with the shadows of the cove, much less the canoes that lay motionless like so many logs on the beach.

The ship passed, and the Indians stood up in their canoes, watching as it disappeared from sight, then turned to resume the attack. The dark ship trembled. Enough water had come in with the now rapidly advancing tide to begin to lift. Two feet of water was not enough to place the ship upright, though, and the attackers were closing in.

"All right, when I give the word everyone up and give the canoes a volley. Then drop back under cover and reload. Now!"

The suddenness caught the Indians off guard. A volley that drew blood in many canoes, filling the cove with cries of anguish, went unavenged. The warriors on the beach fired their covering fire too late.

They were ready now. Surprise wouldn't be achieved again, but the canoes hesitated while the situation was being reevaluated. The ship lurched again.

Captain Beasely shouted again. "The ship isn't going to float in time, but maybe we can drag her upright with the anchor. You men down there, fire into the trees whenever you see a savage. The rest of you—to the capstan!"

The volley roared, puffs of smoke drifted over the deck, and men raced to the capstan. If only the anchor would hold, and if the keel would dig into the gravel, they might get the ship up to where the cannon could be used.

Never before had Jack seen this crew work so hard. He was astonished. The anchor slipped, then held and stopped. Jack ran to the capstan to help. It turned slightly and the ship groaned. He could hardly hear it above the wild yells of the canoers.

Slowly, the masts were moving skyward. The deck was still sloping when they could move the ship no more. To Jack, all the effort seemed in vain.

"That's enough, lads, to the cannon!"

Quickly the lines and canvas were thrown off. As the first of the canoes reached the side of the ship, two cannon snouts poked through the gunwale and roared. They would not depress enough to reach the near canoes, but grapeshot left two on-coming ones a smoking mess of carnage.

Arnold struggled to reload one cannon, Andrew Bloar the other. Albert Arnold had served as a gunner in the Royal Navy before deserting, and he knew how to handle a cannon. Bloar didn't, and in his effort to hurry, he forgot to sponge the barrel before ramming the next charge down the muzzle. It ignited, and in a roar, his face and hands were badly burned. As it was, this may also have saved his life, for in his haste he failed to see a savage climbing in through the port, aiming a spear at the gunner's back. The Indian caught the full force of the premature blast and fell screaming into the water.

Arnold's cannon roared again, and another canoe was destroyed. Those that were climbing aboard were thwarted by the boarding net. Obliged to climb over it, they were easy prey to musket or cutlass. Cavandish was sadistically delighted. "That's it, ye heathen lads, show your bellies for me cutlass to work on ye."

Suddenly it was over. The Indians must have realized that it would not be an easy job to plunder this ship. Their canoes limped away with those who had not gone to Memaloos Illahee. The vessel floated in a cove that was once again every bit at peace.

They left and sailed farther north, avoiding Nootka sound because of the Spanish fort. The dark ship stopped in Kyuquat, however, the next sound north of Nootka. Other ships had traded there but not recently. Every where they stopped, they were greeted with "Waa'com'" or Waa'cush." Some called out "Nuck'y quan," which means "plenty of skins." In this land Jack learned that "Cas mo tee a cong?" meant "What is the name for that?" With this discovery he was able to add to his vocaulary more efficiently.

Jack Ramsay came to be on excellent terms with the Indians of Kyuquot. He conversed with them, learned where their hippahs or places of defense were located, which chiefs could be trusted, and generally gained their friendship. He also learned that they would as soon raid a ship for booty as trade if they could catch the vessel's crew unawares; they found that Jack would as soon join them. This was something both would remember if he came this way again, but now Captain Beasely was much too cautious. The nearly successful attack had been too recent.

Jack could not escape during this trip. The hold was nearly filled, and Captain Beasely was again becoming impatient. One day he suddenly announced, "All right lads, weigh the anchor and set sails. We are China bound."

Eight

"We of the Nehalems called Lamazee's ship Polaklee, meaning the dark one. After Polakle left, pestilence broke out. A disease spread through the coastal villages. Nehalems, Clatsops, Chinooks, and Killamuks suffered alike." It brought high fever and painful sores that left scars on the bodies of the survivors. Our herb medicines and charms had no effect. The Indian practice of casting out evil spirits by sweating in a steamy lodge and running out and leaping into the river only served to further weaken the stricken. Many died.

Loatle the medicine man claimed that the spirits were offended by the coming of the bear people and climbed up Neahkanie Mountain where the gods dwell in order to make peace with Talapus. His pilgrimage made no difference, and since the bear-people were not there when the disease broke out, the Indians had trouble connecting the two. Through the fall, illness continued, and by the time of the salmon run, nearly every lodge of the Nehalems had lost loved ones. Finally, for a reason the natives did not understand, the gods were appeased. The sickness had run its course.

Loatle claimed he had finally found the right charms. Lemolo, untouched by the pox, claimed that the red-haired man-god had willed that she not be stricken. Though not many believed Loatle, even fewer accepted Lemolo's reasoning. Most of the Nehalems forgot the redhead and any mystique about him. Lemolo, though, remained enamored with his memory.

Through the winter suitors came to call on Lemolo and to offer gifts to her father, Shilthlo, in exchange for Lemolo's hand. Some of the gifts were sufficiently large that Shilthlo could remain fairly comfortable during his declining years. He became impatient when she refused suitor after suitor.

Years before, Tsealth, a slave woman who had long since died but who was reputed to have been able to see into the future, forecast that Talapus, the mighty, would come to live amongst the Nehalems. The human form that Talapus would take would have hair like fire, would rise out of the sea, and would take Lemolo as his bride. This became the girl's dream. When pressured by her father, she reminded him of the prophecy and that their lodge was spared by disease. Ramsay, she said, was really Talapus, but he was testing the Nehalems and was not ready to fully reveal himself. Shilthlo was hesitant to enforce his will —yet.

Throughout the winter Lemolo, with her tales and other tricks, held out against all suitors. Spring came early and warm, and it was mating time for the birds and animals of the Nehalem region. The spring salmon migration was bountiful, and an ample supply of huge fish hung on all of the village's drying racks. It was a festive, happy time during which many gifts were received and many daughters given in marriage. Lemolo's father pledged that his patience had ended and that he would exchange Lemolo's favors for a generous gift. He let this be known in the village, and the bidding began.

Each offer, it appeared, was greater than the previous one. Finally, Wautatkam, an older, wealthy man, offered six fine dogs, a dozen fur robes, a fine new fishing canoe, two slaves, and sufficient bits of copper and iron to serve as exchange in gambling for many years. This Shilthlo could not refuse, and Lemolo was told to go with the women of the lodge to purify herself for marriage.

Lemolo tried stalling. She tried frightening Wautatkam with her tales. He seemed unconcerned about the wrath of a red-headed boy. As soon as he had finished a new lodge, they would be married.

Into the midst of this tension, the dark ship sailed again. Lemolo hailed the vessel as an omen, crying out loudly as the dark masts and grey sails swept in through the breakers and the ship made its way up the river to the village. Surely, the ship's arrival before the wedding meant that Lemolo was intended for the red-haired one, and not Wautatkam.

Lemolo's opinions were not widely accepted in the village. Loatle's preachings about the plague were well remembered, and as the ship anchored in the bay, he was gesturing and wailing that the illness was returning. It was Lemolo who faced the medicine man, pointing out that the sickness had occurred in the absence of the bear-people and that none was in evidence as the ship returned to the bay. She won no victory, only a delay. The Nehalems would wait and see. So would Lemolo's father. The marriage to an angry Wautatkam would be postponed—for now.

As trading resumed, mutterings continued in the village. Lemolo resumed her interpretations of Ramsay, saying that if he had been there, his spells would have kept the disease away. Only Loatle and Wautatkam disputed her; the others still waited.

It was apparent with the return that Jack had gained some confidence and self-determination. The experience he gained trading in the northern regions had helped him to become more aware of the Nehalem customs. He worked hard and began to make friends among the villagers. If Jack were ever to escape from the accursed black ship, this might be the place, and the time could be soon.

One young Nehalem, Otallie, a boy about Ramsay's age, was his companion on many occasions. Jack also showed an interest in Lemolo, much to the chagrin of Wautatkam and Shilthlo. Jack's limited signs of interest, though, smiles, quick glances, an occasional word, thrilled Lemolo. In an effort to win her father over to her viewpoint, she began to ply him with tales of Jack really being a chieftain and having great wealth hidden within the dark ship. He had much more to offer, she insisted, than Wautatkam. At first her father ignored these claims, but her instistence and his greed began to pluck at his curiosity. He wondered.

Yakala stated that he was not fooled by this talk. He had observed that Jack Ramsay was actually a slave. He knew this well, for he, Yakala, had owned several slaves himself. He also knew that the bear-people of the sail canoe treated their slaves badly. He was certain that he had heard Ramsay crying out in a childlike manner while others laughed. The boy's cries had drifted across the water as the ship lay anchored at night.

Yakala said the white men of the dark ship once had another slave, and told this story of him.

As the leaves unfolded with the fullness of summer the white men sailed away again. This time they went in the direction that Kalakala-ha, the goose, goes in the winter, Yakala related, pointing to the south. The white men were not gone as long on this trip. They returned before the summer leaves turned the color of the setting sun, even before the small dog-salmon had come to the river.

When the men of the dark ship returned, they had no furs, but had a chest of yellow metal objects. The bear-people also had a new slave, a big man, one with skin as dark as the raven's feather, and whose hair stood out upon his head like a thick huckleberry bush. Although the hair was dark like that of the Nehalems, it was not straight, but wound tightly in little twists so the strands were lost in each other.

Yakala wondered what the bear-people had traded to obtain the box of yellow metal and the dark slave. When the opportunity presented itself, he approached Lamazee about it. Jack had been in the cabin serving his master and had overheard a conversation that he related to Yakala. The captain had said, "I am worried, Jacob, I really don't think we should keep the gold aboard the ship."

"Are you that concerned for your life at the hands of your black-hearted crew?" Smythe laughed.

"Yes, that is a concern to me, and it would be to you, too, if you understood the likes of these men. But that isn't my main concern. Just last week we were hailed by his Majesty's Ship, *CHATHAM*. If they hadn't been in a hurry to stay with the other ship, and if I hadn't the mind to answer in Portuguese, we might well be headed for the execution dock right now. We were lucky, as it were, to be chastised merely for not showing our colors.

"And furthermore, his Catholic Majesty isn't entirely inactive in these parts. The Spanish ships pass here on their way to Nootka Sound, and if they were to decide to board us, they'd know in a moment where we got the gold, and we'd have been better off hanged."

"Don't ye think ye are over concerned, Cap'n?" Symington interjected.

"No, I damned well don't. All it takes is one sharp lookout to spot our masts in here, and any one of them could come in and take us. If they find the gold on board, it will go a lot worse on us than just not having a charter to trade."

"Aw, Cap'n, our dark rigging blends in with the trees beyond the bay. Besides, what else can we do with it?"

"We can take it ashore and bury it."

"The savages would be diggin' it up before ye could row back to the ship."

"Not if we leave the big black fellow there to guard it."

Jacob Smythe laughed. "He'd as soon take it as the savages. Think of all the squaws he could get with what's in that chest. He'd head for the mountains and be set for life."

Captain Beasely leaned forward, an evil gleam in his eyes, and said furtively, "Not if he's dead, he wouldn't."

That took the laughter out of trader Smythe, and he sat, drinking from a bottle of spirits and thinking for a prolonged time. "That might work. These people are a superstitious lot. If we laid him out on the chest with a lot of gestures and mumbo-jumbo and put a cutlass in each dead hand, you couldn't get those Indians to go near the place. Besides, they don't know what we 'ave in the chest. We could say it was a dead crewman's corpse."

Yakala watched as the three chiefs and the black man rowed ashore with the chest that very afternoon. Curious, he took a canoe, crossed the bay, and followed silently through the forest as the four struggled up the hillside with their heavy load. At a safe distance he watched as they bade the big man dig a deep hole. Then they lowered the chest into the pit and motioned for the black man to pack earth around it. As the slave bent over to do this, the captain, who was behind him, struck a blow with his cutlass that nearly severed the black man's head from his shoulders. As he lay quivering and bleeding upon the box, the chiefs turned and made utterances and gestures toward all the trees in the forest. Then they placed a cutlass in each dead hand and covered all with earth and limbs.

In time Yakala told the others of the tribe about the box and the dead slave, but fearful that someone might disturb the soul of this strange dark being and bring a curse upon the tribe, he never told where the chest was buried.

So it was that Yakala had come to believe that Lamazee must have suffered many indignities and abuses at the hands of the cruel masters.

The dark ship stayed a while longer. They traded for furs and provisions: dried fish and clams, jerky, pemmican, and some of the roots they had learned to eat. The crew worked on the ship, repairing various parts, making new wooden limbs for the trees, and rigging a new sail. At times they cooked some black substance they called tar, sending black, evil-smelling smoke drifting up the valley where it frightened the game away. They also took the ship into shallow water where the Nehalems gathered clams. For two days the people could not dig in the clam beds, for the bear-people lay their big canoe on one side, then the other, and worked on it, keeping all the villagers away by threat of their thunder-clubs. When they had finally moved the ship, they left upon the clam beds piles of stinking weed and growth they had scraped from their canoe and pieces of sticky pitch they had spilled.

The Nehalems were angry. There were problems among the bear-people, too. Their chiefs had become increasingly fearful of other ships sent by the great chief of their land which Ramsay said lay across the sea. The great chief did not know this group of bear-people was here, nor did he want them here. They were not obedient tribesmen and feared the great chief's warriors who came in even larger, more powerful canoes. The bear-people of the dark ship were fearful of going again to the northern lands where they had obtained furs before because the great chief had too many ships there.

Captain Beasely ordered a lookout posted on the sandspit beyond the village. At first there was only a path from the place along the bay where they beached a boat, then they built a low shelter against the wind, and finally they put up a hut which they covered with limbs and sand to hide it from the sea.

But there were not sufficient furs to be had from the Nehalems alone, and the trading goods were no longer inducing the villagers to set aside other tasts to seek hides. They dared not venture to where the otter were abundant as the other ships did, but they could trade along the local waterways.

As Ramsay later told his friends, the ship moved north to where a great watercourse broke through the coastal mountains. This proved to be a river, and for a while the traders moved up the river, stopping at various small villages along the way. There they obtained beaver skins, some river otters and foxes, but no sea otters. Still, these peoples were unaccustomed to traders so Smythe was able to make some very satisfactory deals. In addition, the villagers promised to have more skins as the ship returned downriver.

The traders moved on up the river, past low delta land where two rivers joined, then on up into more mountainous country. Though more furs were obtained, the villages were small and, at times, far apart. In addition, the river became treacherous, with strong winds, shallows, and finally cascades. They also found the Indian bands disposed to aggression and stealing. This portion of the trip had been disappointing.

Returning to the delta area, the ship moved up the other river which also showed great volume and was probably navigable for many leagues. The tribes along its banks seemed no larger, but they heard of larger populations in the rich valleys ahead. There was promise of a successful trip as they threaded the tortuous channels that led to the open valley above. Jack had been having difficulty understanding these Indians because they spoke a slightly different tongue, but he was improving his knowledge. They also seemed to be peaceful, simple folks. The crew relaxed.

On the second morning of the journey up this new river, they were still seeking the inner valley. Timbered ridges closed down to the water's edge, and sheer rock bluffs dominated many islands and points. The river floor was rocky in places, swept with fast current rushing over gravel bars in others. At times, lines were run to shore and the capstan used to gain progress, and on two occasions Captain Beasely and Roger Symington shouted angrily as the keel dragged on gravel bars.

By noon, the gravelly area seemed, at least temporarily, left behind, and adequate water surged through a channel bounded by rocky bluffs on each side. As near as Jack could tell, this was the place that the Indians said they must go through to reach the inner valley.

Trickles of water came cascading down the bluffs at intervals. Ahead, a larger waterfall must be waiting, for a dull roar could be heard. Two Indians were taking a canoe out of the water at a trail on the port side.

"Falls ahead on the starboard side." The voice of the lookout seemed more a comment than a warning.

"Steer a bit more to port," Beasely reacted.

"There's some on the port side, too." The lookout was more insistent.

"Where's the channel?" bellowed the captain.

"In the middle, I guess, sir. I mean, I can't make it out."

The captain ran up to the bow as the ship threaded slowly into a swirling force that swept from a horseshoe-shaped cascade. Ahead, an unbroken encircling wall of rock and water stood higher than the decks.

"Blimey, there ain't no channel, Captain."

On the port side, high on the rocks, two Indians paused as they carried their canoe along and looked back at the huge sail canoe.

"Drop the bower! We'll see if there is a way around."

There was not. The Indians took for granted the need to portage around these great falls. Above them, a quiet river stretched for miles in a rich valley peopled by several sizeable tribes.

Captain Beasely had the ship lowered back down from the fast water and moored to rocks on shore. For several days they remained and traded with the local groups and with those who chanced to pass by. But he was not willing to risk sending a party far enough upstream to be out of touch with the ship overnight. He was too accustomed to the attacks of the northern coastal Indians. These Indians, however, did not seem to be nomadic people, and there were few passersby to trade with.

Within a week the frustration had returned, and Captain Beasely was ready to head back downstream. To add to his consternation, the lower river Indians had not gathered as many furs as he felt they should have and he complained bitterly of their indolence. With the hold less than full, they were faced with the choice of wintering on this coast in the face of increasing danger or returning with little profit except their hazardous cargo of gold.

Perhaps they should lay out a village and bastion on the shore and hide the ship.

As the fall leaves began to drop and the call of Kalakalahla, the migrating goose, announced the coming of the first storms, the dark sail canoe again appeared at the land of the Nehalems. Wild cries interrupted life in the village, and Nehalems began running to the canoes. Furs that had been piling up in the lodges could now be exchanged. Whoever arrived at the ship first would have the pick of knives, hatchets, beads, and other wealth.

By the time the anchor was dropped, canoes were alongside. Not waiting for an invitation, many who had been aboard the vessel before climbed onto the ballards, then onto the deck. Captain Beasely was in a foul mood. So was Jacob Smythe, who had just exchanged sharp words with him over the rough crossing of the bar. Mr. Smythe had attributed the rolling to the captain's selection of a passage too far south into shallower water where the swells broke. Smythe had also spilled rum over his trouser legs when the helmsman was obliged to spin the wheel sharply to keep the ship off the beach dead ahead.

Into this atmosphere of hostility and frustration swarmed the gleeful, noisy Nehalems. The first one aboard had been little noticed in the activities of anchoring. This was Jack's friend, Otallie, a stocky, square-jawed lad with solemn face and quiet voice. His straight, shoulder-length hair partially obscured his face as he stood near the rail, hand on Jack's shoulder greeting his red-haired friend. In his solemn way, he was glad to have Jack return to the village.

The next Indian had his hands firmly clenched on the rigging and, with a bundle of furs slung on his back, was about to swing aboard, when a string of loud and abusive profanity from Symington sent the man sliding wide-eyed back to his canoe. On the other side of the ship, several men were coming over the gunwale and starting to run about the deck looking for Smythe to start trading. Jacob Smythe, however, was below getting his rum-soaked trousers off.

Symington, joined by a scar-faced crewman, Harry Parker, began chasing the running Nehalems about the deck, the pitch and volume of profanities increasing. Captain Beasely, bellowing like a bull, joined in the chase, started to pursue one, switched to another as an Indian crossed his path, then started for a third. Crewmen in the rigging, furling sails, either stared in amazement or worked more diligently, fearful of harsh discipline.

In the trader's absence the whole tumultuous gathering came to a focus upon Lamazee. Other than a few trade words Smythe had learned, none of the ship's company had bothered to learn the language of the Nehalems, and no Indians, save Yakala, had learned the speech of the bear-people. Thus, they naturally sought to set things a-right.

Parker, who had been seeking to impress the captain of late, may have been, in his eagerness, the first one to sieze a Nehalem roughly and throw him over the side; it could have been Symington. Several were removed in this undignified manner and separated from their furs in the process. Then the Indians became angry, shouted back insults, and began to resist. There were now as many Nehalems as bear-people aboard, and tempers were flaring on both sides. As Andrew Bloar came down from the rigging, Tyeloha was standing in his way, his back to Bloar, and shouting invectives at Symington. Bloar siezed Tyelaho by his hair and shoulder and pitched him aside. He may have intended to put him over the side into the bay, but he merely sent the man sprawling.

Tyelaho was war chief. As he rose from his ungraceful pose, he was shouting for war, and the Nehalems rallied. They were silent now, and though armed only with the knives that they carried under their cloaks, they prepared to face a foe that had insulted them.

It is doubtful that the white men understood Tyelaho's commands, but they sensed a change in the atmosphere. Captain Beasely gave commands also. The arms locker was opened, and the Nehalems faced different odds. The bear people were outnumbered, but the row of advancing crewmen was armed with the war clubs that called upon thunder and lightning to kill their prey. The Nehalems had seen the deer and elk fall before these things.

Just as Beasely was giving orders to fire, Lamazee sounded the warning. Scrambling quickly, the Nehalems—and Lamazee—leaped over the side. The shots went wild.

Some of the Indians scrambled into canoes and paddled swiftly to shore. Since the beach was close, others elected to swim to safety. Lamazee found no canoe convenient so he continued to swim though he was not very adept in the water. He was untouched by the occasional shooting into the water from the ship, but he was exhausted from his efforts as he reached shallow water. Lemolo was there to help him to his feet, proclaiming him as the red-headed god that had risen from the sea now come to join the Nehalems.

Lamazee, however, had other concerns than the prattlings of this girl. His friend, Otallie, was not to be seen. His eyes searched the shore, and he waded back into the bay where two wounded Nehalems were still being helped ashore. Finally, it was one of the canoers that found Otallie, drifting lifelessly below the surface. They drew him from the water, carried his form ashore and rolled him over a log. No matter how hard they pushed on his chest to expel the water, though, they could not cause Otallie to regain his breath. Lamazee had lost his only close friend.

For a while the red-headed one sank in dark despair, sobbing and wailing like a child. Then he stood and swore vengeance upon the bear-people in the dark sail canoe.

Lemolo was ecstatic. "See," she told all who would listen, "the prophecy of Tsealth is come true. And I will be his bride." The village wasn't ready to accept, however, that this wet and bedraggled youth was a god.

Nine

The evening was quiet. The Nehalems stayed away from the water's edge where the lightning of the war clubs might reach, Lamazee was taking refuge in the bushes behind the Nehalem lodges in a quite ungodlike manner, and the first rain of the oncoming storm was falling. Across the bay, as yet unruffled by the winds that were to come, the creaking of the pulleys was heard, then a shouted command. Braves on shore gripped their knives and war clubs, crouching beside lodges or beneath the crests of dunes. From behind the ship, a boat appeared with many paddles stroking. Was this the attack?

The paddling stopped as the boat came under the bow of the ship. A thick rope was lowered from the ship to the boat, then stretched toward the far side of the bay. More creaking, this time deeper and throatier, then the great anchor began to rise. The men in the boat rowed hard—away from the village. They were towing the ship across the channel, placing greater distance between it and the lodges. The bear-people feared attack as much as the Nehalems.

Night and the rain settled into the valley of the Nehalems. The wind forced raindrops to seek out the cracks in the lodges and people to search for the warmest and driest spots near the cooking fires. All was quiet save for the wailings of mourning squaws and Lamazee. As the cooking fires dwindled, even this ceased. The only sounds were the wind blowing through the tall fir trees and rain dripping from the roofs of the lodges. Tomorrow they would place Otallie to rest amongst the dunes on the sand spit and plot vengeance for his death, but tonight the Nehalems slept.

Dark clouds still scurried across the dark sky as the morning dawned, but the rain had ceased. Gusts of wind stirred the puddles. It would be a suitable day for Otallie's burial.

The cooking fires were scant this morning. Their little puffs of smoke were quickly dispelled by the wind. The Nehalems were mourning. The chanting of the mourners was soft at first, increasing in intensity as feelings ran high. What began as sadness in the morning air grew to heartache in the youth's family. Then, as the chanting and wailing increased in tempo, the hearts of the villagers hardened with hatred. Outside of the circle of the heavy-hearted, small groups of braves talked of war. Into one of these groups Lamazee wandered.

"I will help you with your revenge," he stated. "Otallie was my friend."

For a while Lamazee was ignored. Then, one of the husky men turned to the frail-appearing boy and chided, "What could you do, little one?"

Lamazee thought for a moment. Another stocky man chuckled, "Perhaps he could cast a spell on his friends, the bear-people."

"Yes," answered Lamazee, "I could cast a spell."

Disdainful low grunts followed, then, "Better leave that to Loatle, the medicine man."

Silence fell upon the group as Otallie's body was lifted into his father's arms to be borne to the place of burial. Lamazee turned to follow.

"A moment, red one, what spells can you cast? Can you cast a spell upon the bear-people's war clubs that strike with thunder?"

Lamazee thought for a moment. "Yes," he answered, "if I can get to them."

The group spoke no more as they followed the mourners to the place in the west where the dunes overlooked the breaking surf. There, facing toward the sea that had given the Nehalems the fish of life, the salmon—and the black ship of death—they laid Otallie to rest. There he would remain, where he could watch for the salmon to return and where the gods of Neahkanie Mountain could watch over him.

As the men withdrew to leave the wailing to the squaws, one of the braves resumed the conversation. "How would you cast the spell?"

"With some water," replied Lamazee, who had been thinking of his revenge. "The hard part will be for me to get to the war clubs without the bear-people seeing me."

Lamazee knew that against the muskets and cannons many Nehalems would die if they tried to storm the ship. He had seen other Indians cut down with musket and cutlass as they tried to get past the boarding nets, and he had seen whole canoes laid waste with one cannon blast. He shuddered as he remembered Captain Beasely's boast about nearly severing the black man's neck with one blow. The Nehalems wouldn't stand a chance in a direct assault.

Pausing at the shore of the bay, the little group, Lamazee and the braves, stood looking out at the ship, bobbing slightly fore and aft. Small white-caps, spawned by the winds, swirled about in the expanse of water between shore and the ship.

"Halloo!" Someone on board was shouting. "Ramsay! Jack Ramsay, are you there?" It was Smythe.

Lamazee stood for a moment, conceiving a plan. Then he raised his hand and acknowledged the shout.

"Come aboard, lad, and fetch your friends for some trading."

He needed more time to plan. "The water's 're too rough," he answered, but he was shouting into the wind. He wasn't understood.

"What?"

"The bay. Too rough!" he shouted back.

Silence. He was still not understood. Then he noticed someone, probably Captain Beasely, looking at them with a telescope. Lamazee pointed to the canoes on the beach, then to the water, making large wave motions. The man with the telescope apparently understood. He turned and spoke with the other men on the ship.

"We'll send the longboat to fetch you!"

Jack's heart sunk. He stepped back a few paces.

"What is it, red one?" asked a Nehalem.

"A canoe from the dark ship comes to get me."

Growls emanated from the group as they left to gather knives and war clubs. They would arouse the tribe. From within a lodge a man emerged with a bow and quiver of hunting arrows.

Ramsay knew that they could overpower the crew members in the open boat, but he also knew that the cannons would then lay waste to the village. Many of these people would join Otallie in the sands of the dunes, forever facing west. Perhaps he should run and hide. Jack turned, but in doing so, he looked in the direction where they had just buried Otallie.

"No, let them come! I must go with them to cast my spell. If you come to trade tomorrow I will have taken the thunder from the bear-people's war clubs. Come with furs, but hide weapons to bring aboard."

The longboat arrived, stopping well out in the shallows to the dismay of some of the more aggressive Nehalems. It would be difficult shooting arrows that far into the wind with any degree of accuracy.

The blood-debt would have to wait.

Reluctantly, head bowed, Jack waded to the boat.

"Come on, damn ye, hurry it along. I don't like the looks of yer friends."

He climbed aboard and the red mop of hair disappeared beneath the gunwale. Lamazee sat in the bottom of the boat. Hastily the men rowed out into the bay, pulling against a wind that sought to sweep them up the river. The Nehalems watched as the boat bobbed in the spray, was carried by wind and current upriver to the ship, then came slowly along side.

For a while the watchers could see the red-headed one on the deck. One moment he slipped from the circle of bear-people, appeared at the near corner of the after cabin, then was cornered and siezed up. They tied Lamazee to one of the tall trees of the sail canoe, from where his cries and boyish sobs could be heard across the waters as they whipped him.

Even as night fell the figure of the red-headed one could be seen tied to the tree. The Nehalems knew Lamazee was a slave and was paying a terrible price in order to work his spells. He might even be dead.

In the darkness the man on watch, tired of hearing Jack's sobbing, cut the ropes that held him, allowing him to crawl away and hide. When the sobbing quieted, the crewman gave the boy no further thought. Jack had disappeared below deck, and the man cared not where. It was probably clear to the bilge where he could hide in the ballast.

The crewman was right. Jack went to the bilge, but he had other thoughts than hiding, for now. He soaked his torn clothing in the water that seeped there then carefully returned between decks.

The row of muskets was secured by a chain and immense padlock. To try to break this would arouse the watch. But the spell would be with water, and now. At each upright musket, Jack squeezed a fair amount of water from his saturated clothes, dribbling several spoonfuls down the muzzle so it could soak into the charges of the loaded pieces. Then he dripped more into the priming pans and carefully wiped away any water that showed. To be certain, he returned later and repeated the process. On his third trip to the bottoms he stayed there.

Jack dozed fitfully, uncomfortable from his bruises and cold in his damp surroundings. He was also fearful that his deed would be discovered.

Increasing activity on deck signalled that dawn had arrived. While the crew ate the ship was checked. Jack waited tensely for someone to discover the state of the muskets.

Above him a hatch opened, letting blinding light into Jack's refuge. Legs, then a torso, shoulders, and peering head came through the hatchway, partially blocking the light.

"Jack!"

He didn't answer though a stone rattled as the boy drew lower.

"Jack! Come, lad, get into better clothes. Your Indian friends are coming to trade." It was Jacob Smythe, who had flogged him so soundly the night before for running away. "Here, get out of those wet things."

Stiffly, Jack pulled himself from the wet ballast and followed Smythe up through the hatch. His right leg was numb, causing him to limp as he approached the clothes Smythe had dropped on the planks.

Jack dressed hurriedly but waited for the sounds of bare feet before going on deck. He waited, but none were heard. There were voices, but they were all the crewmen's, Captain Beasely's, or Smythe's. Then Smythe appeared at the ladder. "Get up here. Your friends seem hesitant to come aboard."

Climbing the ladder, then emerging through the companionway, Jack was blinded by the sunlight. It was a clear day, and the wind had died down. He stopped, shading his eyes, then moved to the rail. Several canoes were alongside, loads of furs apparent, but the paddles were still. Other canoes lay in the water near the shore, not moving, waiting for some signal.

Jack looked down at the canoes. He waved. Tyellaho waved his arm, and the canoes moved to the ship. The canoes near the shore were coming, too.

Jack looked about, studying the situation. Smythe had a table set up on deck with a few trade goods arrayed. Sacks behind him probably contained more merchandise. On the after deck Cavendish and Arnold lounged against the rail, muskets cradled in their arms. Forward, near the anchor windlass, were Parker, Bloar, and Edward Morgan, a dark, swarthy fellow who seldom spoke but had an evil look about him. They, too, were armed with muskets. Captain Beasely and Roger Symington leaned on the gunwale behind Smythe. Jack surmised that the cook and the other three seamen were standing by beneath the deck, probably near the arms locker. Jack felt a cold chill as he wondered if the wet charges had been discovered.

Tyellaho and the men of the first canoe came aboard and stood looking about the ship. Nothing was said. Tyellaho looked at Lamazee who nodded his head. Men from another canoe were coming aboard as Tyellaho walked to the trading table and began examining the trade goods.

"Let's see your furs," Smythe said, motioning to the bundle still under Tyellaho's arm.

No response. Tyellaho and several Nehalems went on looking but not approaching close enough for Smythe to get his hands on the furs.

"Jack, come here and get some trading going with your damned friends," Smythe snarled.

For the first time, Ramsay felt a surge of defiance. "They want to start trading with the skins that were left here when the men were thrown overboard."

"What skins?" Smythe snapped. "Nobody left any skins here."

Other canoes had arrived so there were nearly thirty Indians on deck or climbing the side. Symington, seeing the numbers, looked uneasy and whispered something to Captain Beasely. Smythe, who overheard the whispered comment, looked up, then around at the Nehalems. "Jack, you red-haired son of a dock-side whore, you get over here and tend to business, or I'll cut your ears off!"

Jack headed to the table. As he did so, one of the Nehalems reached for one of the sacks behind Smythe. With a quick movement, Symington whipped out a belaying pin and struck the Nehalem down, sending him sprawling senseless to the deck.

"You filthy, thieving, damned . . ."

He never finished the sentence, for another Nehalem drew a short spear from his fur bundle, and in a flash was upon the mate, thrusting the weapon through the man's body. Symington turned to his assailant with an astonished look, then slid to the deck, clutching the shaft of the spear, the belaying pin falling from his hand and rattling across the deck.

Captain Beasely was almost as fast, drawing a pistol from his belt and dropping the warrior with a shot through the temple. Reaching around, he stretched a hand into the sack the first Nehalem had started to pick up, and with drew a cutlass. He never got to use it, however, for a war club crushed his skull before he could straighten up.

Smythe leaped up, overturned table and chair, and rushed madly for the companionway from which the rest of the crew, armed with muskets and cutlasses, emerged. He avoided the Nehalems, but as he passed, Jack siezed his legs, more tripping then tackling the trader. He struggled free, but his flight was arrested enough for an Indian to come between the trader and the crewmen. A knife was raised to stop him forever.

A musket shot rang out, and the Nehalem collapsed to the deck beside Smythe. Oh, no! Why hadn't the "spell" worked? But there was no turning back, for the Nehalems, or for Jack. Desperately, he grabbed the fallen brave's knife and stabbed Smythe in the abdomen.

"No, Jack, don't!" Smythe was struggling to free himself from the legs of the fallen brave, and to draw a pistol from his trousers. The hammer was hung up in a belt loop, and the more he twisted it, the more the pistol became entangled. "Stop, Jack! Be a good lad and have mercy."

Again and again Lamazee thrust the knife into the trader, spilling his blood upon the deck. Then Smythe gave up on the pistol and found Jack's throat with his hands. The trader squeezed until Jack could not breath, and the boy lost consciousness. The knife, held in a hand now pinned by the trader's knee, slipped from his grasp. Then the weight of Smythe's body nearly smothered Jack, but the grip left his throat. The bent-over trader had become an easy mark for a war club.

As Jack regained consciousness, he could barely move from the weight of Smythe's body. Finally, he freed himself and looked up, fearful of the toll of the muskets. One of the men by the companionway had dropped a fired musket, though, and was fighting with a cutlass. An Indian was retreating, holding a gaping wound in his thigh. The other crewmen by the companionway were using their muskets as clubs, or had already discarded them for the more efficient cutlasses. On the afterdeck, Cavendish and Arnold were fumbling with their muskets, struggling to replace the priming. Several braves had climbed onto the afterdeck and were closing in. It had worked!

Rushing forward, Cavendish and Arnold sought to join the group by the companionway. Arnold was quickly encircled and brought down, but Cavendish, taking advantage of Arnold's plight, dashed across the deck, leaped to the main deck below, and quickly accepted a cutlass from the cook.

As Lamazee looked to the bow, the fighting there was over. Blood trickled from lifeless forms and the braves were heading for the companionway, seeking further coup.

On the main deck four men with cutlasses stood, a formidable force which had already inflicted maiming wounds on all who dared to attack. They stood in a circle of mayhem, unapproachable. In the center of the circle, partially hidden by the companionway, sat the cook, feverishly augering out a wet charge from a musket. If he succeded, he could change the tide of battle.

Jack was the first to think of a solution. He looked up on the mean face of Hugh Cavendish, the seamen that first sexually assaulted him. Turning to the dead trader, Lamzaee carefully untangled the pistol then, pointing it forward with both hands, approached the defenders.

Cavendish turned pale beneath his beard. "For God's sake, no! Ye're a good lad, aren't ye, Jack? Here, give me that pistol."

He uttered no more, for the pistol roared, knocking Jack backward and sending the seaman moaning to the deck. Indians rushed forward with a howl, but were driven back bleeding by the remaining cutlasses. Bows and arrows were being brought aboard, though. What the pistol had started, the arrows would finish. There was one last flailing dash for the companionway then all was quiet on the dark sail canoe.

Otallie was avenged.

Ten

McTavish and McDougal sat silently, listening to their Indian host. When the tale of the massacre ended, all three sat thinking of the stark drama of the situation. In the west, the sun was a brilliant firey oval, slowly slipping into the sea. No words were said as it settled lower, half set, only a crescent remaining, a mere brilliant line, then gone.

"What happened to the ship?" McDougal asked.

"After we took from it what we wanted, we burned it. It lies over there, across the waters of the Nehalem from the village in the shadows between those two points. Tomorrow, when the tides are at the lowest, you will be able to see its skeleton, for its black ribs are yet there."

Why did you destroy it?"

"To hide it so that other bear-people might not make war upon us. Lamazee said that his spells could not destroy all, and that the bear-people were many. He said it would be best that we not let anyone know of this."

"Why are you telling us now? Aren't you afraid we might make war to extract a blood debt?"

"No, you must be told so you do not make war on us. You must know the truth, that it was not our doing. The Nehalems were under the evil spell of Lamazee."

"Do you really believe in his spells?"

"Oh, yes, for Lamazee cast his spells elsewhere, upon other peoples. There was another sail canoe, more spells, and more blood flowed."

The *TONQUIN*! Both partners knew instantly what Yakala was referring to. The unfortunate men of the Astor party who had not stayed with the group assigned to build the fort and trading post at the mouth of the Columbia River had gone on north with the ship that brought them. None had come back—none except Lamazee, and he had not returned to Fort George.

Yakala spoke again. "I must return to my people now, but we will speak again tomorrow. You must know how Lamazee tricked us.

"You are welcome to stay with us. There are many empty lodges in the village, any of which you may use. Or, if you prefer, over there is the shelter that the bear-people from the sail canoe left—there in the dunes behind you."

Turning, the two Scotsmen could make out a small open window and the roof line of a shelter nestled into and hidden by the dunes.

"Thank ye," returned McTavish, "We do nae wish to burden yer people in their times of troubles. The shelter in the dunes will be adequate for our needs."

"I go now, but I will return in the morning." Yakala strode down the dunes toward the stricken lodges of the Nehalems. Despite his burden, he stood erect and dignified, a dignity that was evident despite his stocky build and short logs, a physique typical of the coastal Indians who seemed so well adapted to their canoes.

The partners stood silently, watching until Yakala was out of sight in the village. Then they made their way around the hut to its entrance.

"John, I had the feeling there was more than you said about not staying in the village. Don't you trust them?"

"Oh, I will sleep with my rifle handy, for not all may share the opinions of our friend Yakala. But it is nae my concerns of the village people. Did ye nae notice the way the dogs and the children were scratching? The place is beset with fleas."

"Oh," responded McDougal, unconsciously reaching down to scratch his leg.

The hut was a mere lean-to dug into the dunes, with retaining walls on three sides and open toward the estuary. The roof was built of driftwood covered with thatch and sand. It would be difficult to spot from the sea. Within, it was empty, save a few scraps of paper in one corner.

"What did you find there, M'Tavish?"

"Nothing of importance. Likely some rough survey notes."

"Fine, they will help us kindle a cooking fire."

Little was said as the men prepared and consumed their meal. Both were deep in thought, not so much of Lamazee and the men of the dark unknown ship, but those on the *TONQUIN*. Alexander McKay, who had worked and journeyed with both McDougal and McTavish in their earlier times with the Pacific Fur Company, had been on that ship. McKay had been a friend. He was a magnificent man, a true adventurer who had made both overland voyages to the northwest coast of North America with the explorer Alexander MacKenzie in 1789 and 1793.

Duncan was deep in remembrances of his friend. They had served their apprenticeship in the North West Company at the same time. Together, they had reveled at the annual gatherings at Fort William on the edge of Lake Superior. Both proud Highlanders, they had been drawn to each other in comraderie.

They had discussed their clans, their problems, their privations at the tiny trading posts in the interior, their frustrations at the long apprenticeship, and they had shared the decision to leave the Nor'westers and accept John Jacob Astor's offer. Together, in 1810, McKay and McDougal had become two of the four partners with Astor in the Pacific Fur Company. When the *TONQUIN* had sailed from New York that September, bound for the Columbia River, the two had made the trip together. Had it not been for the problems with Captain Thorn, McDougal might have gone north with the *TONQUIN* instead of McKay.

Duncan could still visualize the *TONQUIN*, a mighty ship of nearly 300 tons, with ten cannon and a crew of twenty. Captain Thorn, whom Duncan despised, had been a tyrant, but a man who maintained his ship with naval efficiency. True, he and Duncan had fought over many things, violent arguments that had provoked Captain Thorn to threats to place McDougal in irons, and the Scotsman to respond with a drawn pistol. It seemed to Duncan that he was constantly defending the clerks and artisans from Thorn's outbursts or trying to quiet the loud singing of the French-Canadian voyageurs.

McDougal recalled how he and McKay had been left behind by the impatient Thorn when the two were hunting for fresh meat in the Falkland Islands. Duncan remembered how hard he and McKay had rowed, for miles he was sure, to catch up with the ship. He wondered, if the *TONQUIN* had not been becalmed, would Thorn have left them? Duncan's face flushed as he thought back on how Thorn had left him again in Owyhee.

The whole trip to the Columbia River had been unpleasant because of Captain Thorn. The contemptuous man had been impatient when they arrived at the mouth of the Columbia in foul weather and ordered boats launched to search for a passage through the breakers. Eight men and two boats had been lost. Then, as the sea calmed, the *TON-*

QUIN had been able to sail right into the river. Truly, Thorn's death had been no loss.

McDougal and Thorn had been openly hostile when it came time for the *TONQUIN* to unload the materials and disembark the workmen to construct Astor's trading post. Thus McKay was the only choice to head the trading party aboard the ship when the *TONQUIN* headed north from Astoria.

Time passed. McDougal and the men at the mouth of the Columbia built a storehouse and residences. The surrounding land was cleared and gardens prepared. Trade was established with the Chinooks across the river, the Clatsops along the coastal plain to the south, and the Wahkiacums and Cathlamets upstream from the post. Still the *TONQUIN* did not return. Trade fell off, and tensions mounted. Quickly the traders and workmen built the bastions, stockade wall, and armory. McDougal, fearing a conspiracy, called the chiefs together and threatened to release a plague of smallpox from a bottle he held should the Indians bring war.

More months would pass before Indians coming from the north to fish for the giant sturgeon of the Columbia would spread tales of the *TONQUIN* massacre. McDougal had still hoped for the safety of his friend McKay. Perhaps the tales could not be believed; perhaps McKay was being held as a slave, and might be rescued. A few other massacre victims had been. Then other Indians, people of the north, told of the siezure of the *TONQUIN*. None of the white men had been allowed to live, they said. Duncan had brooded silently for days. He asked of Lamazee, who had reportedly survived and returned, but the Chinooks said the red-head had gone on south.

Now he sat stunned again, and McTavish, understanding Duncan's feelings, sat quietly. Besides, he had his own personal thoughts. He had known McKay less well than had McDougal, for McKay and McDougal had left the North West Fur Company to work for Astor. McTavish remained with the Nor'westers and had come to this region to be in charge of a trading post in the Wollamet area, the broad valley the dark ship under Captain Beasely had failed to reach because of the falls.

McTavish renewed his friendship with McDougal when he had been sent by the Nor'westers to await the arrival of the *ISAAC TODD* at the mouth of the Columbia. When the ship did not arrive on schedule, McTavish bought supplies from McDougal and returned to the Wollamet post. McTavish returned in the fall, and, at that time, negotiated the puchase of Astoria for the North West Fur Company. He had found McDougal already despondent over the loss of the *TONQUIN*, and the feared loss of another Astor ship, the *BEAVER* (which had not returned from a northerly trading trip). The killing of Pacific Fur Company traders by up-river Indians, and the failure of the supply ship *LARK* to arrive also caused him concern.

A new Nor'wester alliance had been formed. McDougal, McTavish, and another former Nor'wester with the Pacific Fur Company, Donald McKenzie, were together again. Three other Astor employees joined the North West firm, the clerks, Ross, McLennan, and Ross Cox. If only McKay were there.

John was exhausted by the day's journey and events. He sat in a dark corner, nibbled on jerky, then slid down to the soft sand of the hut floor. He was still brooding about the *TONQUIN* tragedy and the fate of Alexander McKay as his eyes closed. Unconsciously, McTavish's hand reached into the pouch and closed upon the warlock stone.

Eleven

The red-headed youth, older now, and wearing a strange costume, stood upon the deck of a ship, his tanned and freckled skin bare from the thigh down, a robe of deer skin covering his shoulders and hanging to his legs. In his arms he held a smaller robe of reed matting, and upon his head rested a conical hat of woven bark. Beneath the headdress hung two tails of oiled red hair. Except for his skin color, the blue eyes, the hair, and the fact that his head had not been flattened in the manner of the coastal Indians, he appeared like one of the savages. Jack, the unwilling cabin boy, had become Lamazee, the Indian.

The ship was different, also. This was not the dark schooner with blackened mast and rigging; this was a larger square-rigged ship with scrubbed decks, white paint on the sides, and polished mahogany railings. It held two rows of cannon, one on each side of the main deck. This was the *TONQUIN*.

Lamazee had come forward and offered to go with the ship as an interpreter. He was the son, he said, of a sailor who had jumped ship and taken up with an Indian woman. Captain Thorn agreed. That would be well, for Lamazee's father had taught him remarkable English, though he spoke with a strange inflection, as though he had a speech impediment. No matter, for the fellow assured Captain Thorn that he had been on trading expeditions along the northern coast before and had learned much of the languages of the northern people. The local language, known as Salish, was generally related to the tongues of the peoples as far north as the great passage to the inland sea. Beyond were the languages of the Nootkas and the Haidas, of which he had learned many words. Thorn was impressed with Lamazee's claimed knowledge.

Alexander McKay had overheard the conversation which had taken place on deck. He objected. McKay didn't like the looks of the Indian and suspected his motives. He had been too eager to get aboard, too agile at swinging over the side, and altogether too familiar with ships. Captain Thorn looked upon all traders, even McKay, with disdain and was insistent that Lamazee accompany the ship now that he knew

McKay objected.

From that moment on, McKay kept a wary eye on Lamazee. How could a savage know where the water barrel would be? Something was amiss. Who was he? McKay was certain Lamazee was not a sailor, for, as the ship got under way and cleared the river mouth and moved into the long ocean swells that sweep into the northwest beaches from the broad ocean, Lamazee was seasick.

The sun shone bright on the June afternoon. A stout north wind, typical of the summer days, blew down the coast. Into this wind the TONQUIN tacked, first well out to sea, straight into the swells, sending an occasional refreshing spary over the bowsprit, then toward shore. As the ship swung to starboard, angling toward the shoreline, it rolled mightily as the swells passed beneath the hull.

Lamazee, McKay noted, knew enough to rush to the leeward rail to relieve his queasy stomach. As he leaned far over the gunwale, the wind momentarily lifted the red-headed savage's skin robe and flung it over his shoulder. Lamazee's back was bare only a moment, but the Scotsman was sure he saw the long scars left by floggings.

McKay discussed this observation with the clerk, Lewis. To them it was apparent that the interpreter was not what he claimed to be. Together, they confronted the captain, but Thorn scoffed at their "evidence" and refused to take them seriously.

They could only wait. The crew and officers feared Captain Thorn too greatly to be seen discoursing with McKay or any of the fur company employees. On this matter the ship's company was much relieved, for only McKay and Lewis remained of the traders. Things were less crowded. There were no longer French-Canadian voyageurs singing their boating songs on the foredeck; McKay lacked other Scotsmen to speak Gaelic with. Tension was lessened, but the crewmen still avoided the remaining traders.

It was not gossip with McKay, as Captain Thorn had maintained, that brought dissent over Lamazee. The men of the crew had grown to dislike the red-head on their own. They had not studied the man as McKay had. With the crewmen it was instinctive. They did not go out of their way to harrass him as the men had on the dark ship but neither did they offer him any comforts. He was left strictly to his own devices as long as he stayed out of the way.

The next two days of northerly sailing were relatively quiet. The stout wind continued to blow down the coast, and skies remained clear. In the evening the wind abated so that all were able to rest at night, save those on watch. Even the interpreter's seasickness had abated; he was once again adjusted to the roll of a ship.

Each morning, before the wind increased in velocity, Captain Thorn decreed that the deck be scrubbed. This activity, on the fourth day out of Astoria, happened to place Lamazee, Alexander McKay, and one of the seamen upon a collision course. As the Company Partner left the after main deck where he had been lounging, he walked along the port side. Lamazee was on the deck and heading for the port rail to get away from the area being scrubbed. Seeing that this would place him right in the path of McKay, Lamazee turned and wandered into an area of freshly scrubbed deck.

The seamen had been grumbling over their captain's insistence that the deck be scrubbed daily and their discontent grew as they talked. The man working closest to Lamazee was seething with anger. Lamazee's "dirty Indian feet" treading on their freshly scrubbed deck was too much. The sailor siezed his bucket and threw the wet, cold contents out upon the deck before him—and upon Lamazee's legs.

Whirling, the red-head gasped and spit out, "Ye scurvy son of a dockside..." Stopping mid-oath, he flushed and spun away from the seaman, but found himself face-to-face with Alexander McKay.

"Hm-m," mused McKay loudly, then, taking a wild chance, said, "Let's see, I would guess it to have been Newcastle-upon-Tyne that you shipped out of. Is that right?"

The red-headed youth stood frozen. He was obviously caught and wanted to run, but McKay was in front of him, and the seaman, now standing, was behind him. His mouth moved as though to utter words, but no sounds came. The sailor was beside him now, looking at the interpreter's arm where a tatoo was faintly visible beneath the tan and dirt. "Jack Ramsay."

It was the captain that saved him—for the moment. "You, Pennington, get back to work! Mr. McKay, Mr. Lamazee, can't you find some other place to visit besides an obvious work area?"

The interpreter quickly stepped around McKay and headed toward the bow, placing the captain between himself and McKay. The trader would have to bide his time for now, but he had the perseverance of a Highlander and would continue the hunt later. Ramsay knew this was likely and wanted to hide in the bilges, but he knew he dare not, for he was an Indian interpreter now and must remain on deck. To hide below would be enough to arouse the suspicions of even the stubborn captain.

McKay walked over to the starboard side where Lewis, the clerk, had gone after emerging from the cabin. The Scotsman related the event to the clerk. He was sure now that their interpreter was a white man mascarading as an Indian, but for what purpose?

"Mr. McKay," asked Lewis, "how could the fellow have gotten to this wild shore? If we could figure that out, perhaps it would suggest what his mischief is."

"Aye, Jamie, I don't think the fellow got here with the Royal Navy survey. He doesn't hae the bearing of one that has been in His Majesty's service, nae that all of our sailors are that fine, but they don't slink around. This one is of a lower cut. From his age he no doobt came here during the time of the sea otter trading. A goodly number of the traders for otter peltries were Americans and most have quit the area now that the otter herds are thinned out. But this lad seems English—or even Scottish. I think I guessed right on Newcastle-upon-Tyne.

"Sometimes Lamazee sounds a wee bit Scottish, but he knows the vocabulary of an English sailor, so I guessed at Newcastle which is near the border."

"But whose charter was he trading under, Mr. McKay? I thought the King had restricted the trading."

"Aye, lad, he did. But there hae been certain merchant venturers that came over here anyway. I would wager, Jamie, that he came here in the otter trade, that he is English, and that he is here illegally. He would wind up at Old Bailey if the Navy caught him here."

"Do you think his ship is about? Would it attack us?"

"No, I do nae think so. The *TONQUIN* is well armed."

"Well, sir, beg your pardon, but could he be a British spy?"

"Not likely. To be a spy requires courage, and Lamazee does nae seem to possess that quality. Most of the time he acts more like a frightened and outcast child.

"No, he must be separated from his ship. I would guess that he has been living among the savages for nigh a decade. Either he deserted his comrades or worse has happened to them."

"Are you going to talk to him some more?"

"Aye, that I am, but I am going to have to catch him away from Captain Thorn."

"Captain Thorn has wanted to go over the inventory of trading goods that were left aboard the ship. Perhaps I could engage him in that task and distract him."

"Good lad! I can nae think of anything he likes to do more than check up on the company's trading goods."

James Lewis waited while the captain finished berating a crewman and until he had completed his morning inspection of the ship. During the pause that followed, Lewis went forward, paper and pencil in hand, and suggested that they begin the inventory. For once the captain was agreeable, and the two left the deck and went below.

As soon as the captain was out of sight, McKay set out to find the interpreter. He found him far up in the bow, ahead of the anchor windlass, squatting on the deck. Lamazee started, but it would have brought suspicion for him to leave. McKay sat down near the windlass, drew out his pipe, and offered some tobacco to the man in Indian garb. The offer was refused with a shake of the head, but McKay held him in his gaze and began a conversation.

"Well, Ramsay, do ye find this ship more to your liking than an English vessel?"

The red-head flushed, wishing to run, but sat paralyzed. He struggled for words, but none came. Looking out of the sides of his eyes, he saw McKay, sitting comfortably by the starboard rail, quietly puffing on his pipe. Lamazee felt held by the Scotsman's steady gaze—the gaze of a man patiently waiting to be answered. In addition, the red-head could hear a group of seamen near the main deck. If he left he would have to go that way, and he feared the sailor he had cursed.

Lamazee sat silently as the trader continued looking and puffing on his pipe. The man was still waiting for an answer. Finally he nodded his head. McKay was breaking through.

"Aye, Mr. Ramsay, this is a right trim ship." McKay looked up into the billowing canvas aloft. Turning back, he continued. "I guessed right, didn't I, that ye sailed from Newcastle-upon-Tyne?"

There was a pause again, then Lamazee nodded his head.

"Well, after all," McKay went on, keeping his voice calm, "fellow Scotsmen ken another's secrets." He was bluffing, but he was going to push as much as he dared. "What was the name of your ship?"

This was obviously upsetting. The red-head squirmed. A muscle twitched in his face as he struggled with his speech. He fumbled with a few sounds, then blurted out, "The Laven."

The Laven? McKay thought he knew all the ships that had been in the otter trade: *FAIRY*, *GRACE*, *GUSTAVUS*, the brig *HANCOCK*, and the other American ships, *WASHINGTON*, *MARGARET*. He was running the names through his mind. He made a mental list of the British ships—there was Captain Moore in the *PHOENIX*, Captain Adamson with the *JENNY*, and there were the *JACKALL* and *PRINCE LEE BOO*. No, he had never heard of a *LAVEN*. McKay didn't understand, but thought he shouldn't press it. Perhaps Ramsay was having a problem with his speech, and it might stop him from talking if the trader said anything that called attention to his problem. He would go on to another question.

"Was it as large as the *TONQUIN*?"

"No—smaller." Lamazee was calming down.

"Was it a bonnie ship?"

"No. Dirty, black with tar, crawling with lats, many fleas."

"I'll bet you were glad to be away from it. Did ye have many friends in the crew?"

"No." The answer was brief, and from the quiver in the voice, McKay could tell he had touched upon a sensitive subject. The Scotsman felt the tense emotions and guessed that this lad with a speech impediment had been terrorized by a harsh crew. The red-head's face momentarily had the expression of a frightened boy, then it quickly returned to the previous sullen countenance.

McKay pressed on. "What happened to the ship and crew?"

The tension, the frightened-boy look returned. Lamazee flushed, sat open-mouthed for a moment, struggling for the sounds. "Gone."

McKay wasn't satisfied with the answer. He was intent now, no longer slowly puffing on his pipe. His teeth clenched on the stem and rapid puffs of smoke drifted off with the breeze. He had his quarry at bay and was moving closer. He played another hunch.

"Were they killed?"

A chill went through Lamazee's body. He might have bolted and run except that the voices of the crewmen on deck were closer. Silently, he nodded.

"Indians?"

Lamazee nodded again.

McKay was getting to the bottom of the story now. "Aye, and why did they nae kill ye?"

The color went out of the interpreter's face. Instinctively his hand reached up and around his throat, as though feeling the choking hands of Smythe, or, more likely, reaching for a hangman's noose that wasn't there yet.

Suddenly they were interrupted by running feet. Two sailors came rushing around them.

"Out of the way, quick, we're going to drop the anchor."

Standing up and stepping away from the anchor chain, McKay could see that they were between an island and the mainland. A steep bluff extended from a rocky beach to a flat area above. Several trails of smoke led his eyes to the roofs of a sizable Indian village.

"Well, Mr. McKay," Captain Thorn's voice rang out, "perhaps we can begin the trading you have come along for."

The forward motion of the ship had ceased, and the anchor chain was paid out. As the sailors in the rigging finished furling the sails, the *TONQUIN* rolled gently in the swells. The sea was relatively calm in the lee of the rocky island, but no Indian canoes came out to greet the traders.

At the mouth of the Columbia, the impatient Captain Thorn had lost both the whaleboat and the pinnace trying to find a safe channel through the breakers. The whaleboat was never seen again, and the pinnace, though washed ashore, was so badly smashed it could not be repaired. Only the longboat remained, but the captain was tired of waiting. He ordered the boat made ready and some of the men to man the oars. It was his intent to send Lamazee and the traders ashore to initiate the exchange.

"Oh, no," responded the interpreter as soon as the plan was made known to him. "Bad people."

"What do you mean Mr. Lamazee?"

"They wait on beach, behind the logs to kill you. It would be better not to try to trade here."

Captain Thorn scowled. They had come here to obtain a cargo of furs. This was the first opportunity for him to command the trading. He was not going to give up easily.

Picking up his telescope, Thorn trained it upon the bluffs. Two steep trails led down the bluff from the village. The route to the beach was relatively open so the captain could see the Indians as they ascended. Yes, they were armed.

For the next ten minutes he continued to watch. He had not yet countermanded his order to prepare to launch the boat, and the crewmen were proceeding as slowly as they dared. The boat was cleared, attached to the davits, and swung over the side.

Finally, the boatswain gave the order, "Lower away!"

"Hold!" the captain commanded, not raising his head from the telescope. McKay, Lewis, and the others stared intently at the beach. They could see Indians but could not make out whether they carried furs for trade or were armed. They could see canoes on the beach, but none were making their way through the breakers.

Captain Thorn straightened up and spoke. "Mr. Lamazee is right. The scoundrels have their canoes pulled up on shore, are armed, and are taking positions behind the logs on the beach. They would be on us in a moment if we landed. Mr. Lamazee, we are obliged to you.

"Swing the longboat in, weigh the anchor, and make sail!"

"Should we give them a broadside for troubling us, sir?" asked one of the officers.

"No, we may find better use for the powder."

The captain walked over to Lamazee, personally thanked him for saving the men and the longboat, then walked off toward his cabin. McKay knew Captain Thorn would be alone, but also realized this was not the time to talk to him about the interpreter. Instead, he stood alone at the rail as the first mate and the crew got the ship under way.

For some time McKay stood at the rail, thinking about Jack Ramsay. He was concerned about the massacre of the crew Jack had sailed with and wondered what part the redhead might have played in the bloodletting. His same inclinations could be applied to those on board the TONQUIN.

The ship was under sail, and the crew members had climbed back down out of the rigging. Two of them stood on deck a short distance from where McKay leaned against the rail. James Lewis passed them as he approached the chief trader.

"Sir, did you find out anything from Lamazee?"

"Yes, Jamie, I found out quite a bit, though not all that I feel we must."

"What is it, sir?" Lewis was intent.

The two seamen had stopped talking and were just barely refraining from turning their heads in the direction of Lewis and McKay.

"Lamazee, or Jack Ramsay if ye prefer, is from an English ship. He said its name was *LAVEN*, I believe, though I was having difficulty understanding his speech."

"*RAVEN*, sir."

"What's that, laddie?"

"*RAVEN* was the name of the ship. Ramsay often uses an 'L' sound for an initial 'R' in a word. You know, Ramsay-Lamazee, Raven-Laven."

"Aye, I believe you are right. He said the ship was black, which would befit the name of Raven."

"Please go on, sir, what else did he say?"

Behind them the two crewmen seemed intent upon some aspect of the rigging, perhaps the end of a spar above the traders, for they had moved closer.

"Not much. They sailed from Newcastle-upon-Tyne, were involved in otter peltries—illegally I would wager."

"But what of them now? Where is the ship and crew?"

"I do nae know of the ship. But the crew is dead. I managed to worm out of him that they were massacred by Indians."

"What about Lamazee? Why wasn't he killed with the crew?" Lewis gasped. "He seems to be one of the bloody savages."

"I could nae find out. We were interrupted by the anchoring so I could nae question him further."

Lewis whirled and started toward Captain Thorn's cabin. "Good heavens, we must go to the captain!"

"No, Jamie." McKay reached out and stopped the boy. "It wouldn't do any good. Right now the captain thinks highly of Lamazee for sparing us the clash with those heathens back there. And you know how highly he regards those, like us, in the trading party. We will hae to wait for the right moment."

The two stood at the rail, looking at the wild and savage coastline, thinking in silence. The two seamen wandered away, apparently satisfied with the tackle aloft.

Twelve

"Mr. Lewis! Come, the inventory must be completed." The captain had seen the two traders leaning against the rail. Disdainful of what he considered the laziness of the men in the trading party, he was determined to see to it that at least one would perform some work that he considered useful.

McKay remained at the rail for a few more minutes, long enough for Captain Thorn and the clerk to disappear below deck. Then he set out to find Ramsay. Perhaps he could resume the discussion. He glanced around the deck, but the fellow was nowhere to be seen. McKay wandered forward to the bow, trying to appear casual. He circled a mast, continued forward, and arrived at the anchor windlass. No, Ramsay was not there.

Slowly reversing his direction along the opposite side of the deck, the trader looked over all the obscure places on the main deck. He re-lit his pipe as he wandered aft.

McKay doubted that Ramsay would be near the helmsman, but he walked that way to be certain.

"Another fair day," commented the helmsman as McKay passed.

"Aye," he responded, nodding his head. Well, Ramsay was nowhere on deck. What could the scoundrel be up to?

McKay's attention was diverted to loud words coming from the after companionway. The speakers were coming onto the deck. They were Lewis and the captain. Lewis was red-faced, perplexed, and obviously frustrated. Captain Thorn was his usual sarcastic, abrasive self.

"Now, no more of that, Mr. Lewis. I won't have you causing trouble on my ship. You and your confederate keep your council to yourselves lest I find it provident to put you ashore. It should be obvious to you the service the man can give to us."

"But, captain, if you would only talk with Mr. McKay . . ."

"Enough! The lad, this very day, saved us from those filthy savages who would have attacked us." Thorn was angry.

"Himself he saved! He was ordered to go in that boat."

"Stop it, damn you!" roared Thorn, and Lewis, red-faced, turned and walked toward his superior, whom he had just spotted.

McKay shook his head. He knew that the clerk had disregarded his advice and insisted on discussing Lamazee with Thorn. He had been soundly rebuffed, and now it would be more difficult than ever to convince Thorn of the danger.

At the other end of the main deck, another commotion was occurring. Lamazee was propelled out of the other companionway with an angry seaman right at his heels.

"What goes on there?" bellowed Thorn.

"I don't want the quare fellow around me, sir. I'm not that kind, sir."

For once the captain was caught without words. He hadn't considered this aspect of the interpreter. Thorn had consistently dealt harshly with any behavior that was suggestive of homosexuality. But to censure this man would be to acknowledge that the traders might have been right. He paused, looking quizzically at the sailor, then at Lamazee, who was trying to slink away.

"Aye, sir, he's a bit quare."

Thorn still didn't know what to say. He couldn't let up on the discipline of the crew, but he was still within earshot of his adversaries, the traders.

"You are mistaken, Andrews. You just don't know anything about the customs of the heathens.

"However, it was agreed that you, Mr. Lamazee, were to remain on deck. To prevent any further misunderstanding, I must ask you to remain up here. Do you understand?"

The interpreter stopped and nodded. "I was hungry," he offered as explanation.

"Oh, of course. Well, whenever you are hungry just mention it to one of the officers. He will dispatch someone to find some food for you.

"I hope you have not been offended. This man simply didn't understand what you wanted. He is unfamiliar with your customs and language."

"Captain, sir, what he done wasn't no heathen custom, it was what any horny..."

"That's enough, Andrews. Go below and fetch some victuals for

Mr. Lamazee."

"Aye, lad, Hornie he is," muttered McKay.

"What was that, sir?" asked Lewis.

"Oh, that. In the Highlands, Hornie is the name of Satan."

Captain Thorn waited to see that the task had been accomplished to his satisfaction, then proceeded to check landfalls against his charts. He reckoned they would reach the Strait of Juan de Fuca that night or the next morning.

Lewis was studying Lamazee who was standing with his back to the starboard rail. The redhead's face was not turning but his eyes were following the movements of the crewmen as they worked. Could this strange person, masquerading as an Indian, be in league with satan as McKay had said?

The balance of the day passed without further incident, and that evening they did, indeed, sight the entrance of the broad strait. As the dusk gathered, the captain guided the *TONQUIN* to a sheltered cove of suitable depth for anchorage. Thorn was careful to select a location far enough from shore so that the ship would not be surprised by savages. After the morning's incident, double watch was posted for added security. It was soon apparent, though, that the ship was anchored too far out to be clear of the heavy currents running through the straits. Everyone was astounded by the amount of current in this large body of water and that it extended even to the entrance to the cove where they were anchored. Lamazee, however, assured the captain that this was usual for these northern waters.

With this assurance, a bower was dropped so a second anchor could add holding power beyond the kedge that was originally placed. With this extra precaution the *TONQUIN* settled down for the night. Stars appeared, twinkling brightly at times, occasionally dimmed by puffs of sea mist that drifted with the breeze. The night was pleasant for walking on deck, and Alexander McKay was having an evening stroll before retiring. In the course of this, he came upon the interpreter, who was preparing a sleeping place beneath a spare sail.

"Well, Mr. Ramsay, you certainly warned us in a timely manner today. You seem to ken these heathens quite well."

Lamazee completed his preparations and lay down. He did not respond to the trader.

"Was it the savages of this region that killed the crew of yer ship?"

Ramsay looked up, hesitated, but finally answered, "No, not these people."

"Well, I certainly hope Chief Comcomly's tribe are nae given to such practices. If so, all the men we left to build the post at the Columbia are in imminent danger."

McKay had him. Lamazee knew he had to be specific, for if he wasn't, the trader might sound the alarm and that would be the end of the trading trip. The TONQUIN would race back to Astoria. "No, no. People on the other side of some mountains to the south of there, called the Killamuks. They are strong warriors—kill many, take lots of slaves. They live in several groups, though, none very large. One of these groups, called the 'Halems. They don't go to the great river much, occasionally to trade. They are mostly interested in taking wealth and slaves and will not kill your friends unless they go to lands of the Killamuks."

"Interesting," mused McKay, "if they are so given to killing and slaving, why did they nae kill you?" He was pressing again, hoping for clues as to how much danger the TONQUIN might be in. What could Lamazee be plotting?

"Don't know," responded the redhead, who rolled over as if to go to sleep. Lamazee pulled a mat up and around his head so his ears were covered. McKay was not going to get his answers tonight. This was certain, for Captain Thorn was beginning a nighttime inspection of the ship, and any disturbance with Ramsay was sure to bring Thorn's wrath.

As McKay descended the companionway to his sleeping quarters, a voice called out, "Mr. M'Kay, did you learn anything more?"

Turning, the Scotsman expected to see the clerk, James Lewis. Instead, it was one of the sailors.

"I did nae knew ye were aware of our discussions."

"Reed and Porter overheard you and Mr. Lewis on deck this morning, sir, and everyone could hear Mr. Lewis and the captain. They spoke very loudly and heatedly in the hold. The crew are with you, sir."

"Well, that's comforting to know. However, I did nae learn much more than I told Mr. Lewis. The savages who performed the mischief on Ramsay's ship were to the south of our new trading post if the words of the likes of him can be trusted. However, I still did nae find out why they spared him so I do nae know how much he may have been in league with the murderers.

"The ship he was on was apparently the RAVEN."

"Yes, I remember the ship," a voice joined in as another seaman approached. "I was a British seaman, then, aye, and sailed many a time out of Newcastle-upon-Tyne. That RAVEN was a bad ship, belonged to a bunch of merchants, she did, that would like as cut yer throat for a shilling. I was never on her, but they say she had a mean captain. Some that sailed on her never came back—and finally she didn't."

The first sailor spoke again. "Sir, are we in danger?"

"I can nae tell, not until we find out what this rogue of a false Indian is about."

"Don't worry, sir, we will all keep a weather-eye peeled."

"I have been thinking," came a new voice. It was Jamie Lewis, who had heard the voices and wandered out into the companionway. "Lamazee would have been younger then, perhaps much younger. Indians have been known to spare a child in a massacre. Or, his red hair and manner of speech could have been held in awe by the superstitious heathens. He could be innocent, perhaps not in league with the savages."

"Well, I doobt that, or he would hae been willing to tell us aboot . . ."

"What goes on down there?" It was the captain, silhouetted in the opening leading to the deck. "What are you plotting? If you haven't anything better to do than gossip, Pennington, I can find something for your labors. Who is that with you?"

The second man had disappeared, however, and no one spoke.

"Come and start rigging some spare spars, right now! And you, Mr. McKay, I'll thank you not to meddle in the affairs of my crew."

Thus the speculation ended for the night. Thorn sought to maintain a wedge between the trading party and the crew. But, could he maintain it in the face of sensed danger? Might, instead, that wedge work its way between him and all else aboard, save the distrusted Lamazee?

Thirteen

Early the next morning the lookout sighted canoes rounding a point on the south shore of the strait, heading for the *TONQUIN*. The word had obviously been passed during the evening or morning hours, and now the natives were arriving at the trading ship. The interpreter, however, seemed agitated.

"Lookout, what do you make of it?"

"I don't see any peltries, sir. And I think they are armed."

"All right. Mr. Lamazee, do you speak their tongue?"

"Yes, some, but they are bad people, not good to trade with."

Captain Thorn quietly gave orders to arm some of the crew but stationed them out of the view from the canoes. He also gave orders that none of the Indians be allowed aboard until he gave the approval. In this manner the crew stood ready as the first canoe came along side the ship.

A greeting, then a brief speech came from the leader of the natives. They were a fierce-looking lot, dressed in woolen cloaks and bear skins, tatooed wildly, and armed with an assortment of weapons. One of the Indians in the nearby canoe held a heavy spear with a long, barbed bone point, some had bows and arrows, and all had heavy carved wooden war clubs within reach.

Lamazee turned to the captain, reporting, "They come to ask for pachito—presents. They are Tatooche people, and this man who speaks is a toyon, a chief."

"Ask them if they have furs to give in return."

The interpreter turned, and with halting words tried to convey the captain's meaning to those in the canoe. He first asked for elaka, sea otter in the trade language of the coast to the south. Silent stares were the only reaction. Lamazee then tried a more northern tongue, asking wa'tah nuckky, if they would trade for otter. A few growls ensued, and more silent stares. There was a short, low conversation between the toyon and a man that apparently was in charge of a second canoe that arrived. By their glances up to the deck of the ship, they were obviously displeased with the refusal of their request for pachito.

Turning suddenly to the captain, Lamazee reported, "They attack."

A shower of arrows arched up from the canoes, a few hanging in the rigging, but most thumping into or rattling across the deck. A cry from above told that the lookout had been hit. Captain Thorn ordered the armed men forward and shouted for them to fire. The balance of the crew was dispatched below to be armed.

One of the savages was standing, spear raised, seeking a target when the first volley was fired. A musket ball found its mark in his skull, and he toppled backward into the sea, the first evident fatality of the engagement. Some warriors in the canoes were wounded, but other canoes swept in, determined to press the attack.

Before the men who had fired the first volley could reload, or those who had gone below for arms had returned, these assailants were alongside, discharging arrows and looking for a way to climb to the deck. To return the Indians' fire, the men of the TONQUIN had to show themselves above the gunwale.

Turning to the captain, the first mate suggested, "Sir, wouldn't it be best to drive them off with the cannon so as not to expose the men to arrows?"

Thorn, however, was in his usual negative mood despite the danger. "No, Mr. Carpenter, there are few enough of them that we will save the powder."

The attention of the men at the rail was now diverted from the Indians to Captain Thorn. This was not the first time they had thought of mutiny, but it was the first time they had thought of it when they were armed. Captain Thorn had lost the crew's respect, and the men were unwilling to risk their lives for him. Lamazee sensed the feeling and slunk away to hide behind the far side of a hatch. The other officers also sensed the change in the men and their looks at the captain. They placed themselves between Thorn and the men at the rail.

"You men at the rail," the first mate called, "step lively and present your pieces to the enemy! No, hold your fire. They are moving off."

Attention was diverted to the attackers, who had now plucked their dead comrade from the water and were leaving in the direction from which they had arrived. Others lay still in the bottoms of canoes. There would be wailing at more than one lodge that day. One of those stricken was the man Lamazee had referred to as a toyon, and perhaps that accounted for the withdrawal of the Indians.

The killing of a chieftain normally called for the extraction of an equal or greater blood debt from the enemy. Likely the whole tribe would return to this spot to seek payment. They would be fully armed and determined that blood should flow across the decks of the TON-QUIN. For this reason the crew and trading party agreed with Lamazee's suggestion that they depart this unfriendly coast.

At first Captain Thorn refused. It was not a day for him to be in the mood for agreement. Unrest was growing again as Ramsay further stated that tribes in this area had few furs to trade since they were more interested in making war and taking slaves than in hunting or trapping. It was this, the prospect of wasted time and no profit, that brought Thorn around to the notion of weighing anchor and sailing farther into the strait.

During this disagreement, the wounded lookout had been forgotten. His shouts attracted attention on the deck, and two sailors headed aloft to assist him. The captain did not wait for the wounded man to be lowered and tended. Now that he had made up his mind to sail, he ordered the sails unfurled and the anchor weighed immediately. When the men seemed intent upon the man being lowered to the deck, Thorn swore at them and commanded them to work faster.

Herman Krause, the lookout, had been struck in the lower leg by an arrow. Fortunately, it did not strike the bone, but it did protrude from the leg as help arrived. One of the rescuers cut the shaft off, but did not succeed in removing the arrow aloft. A rope ladder was then tied about the injured man's waist and tossed over a spar. In this way two men could help Krause down the rope ladder while another person on deck held the line, paying it out to keep it taut in case the man fell. He was somewhat faint and having difficulty adjusting to the movement of the ship as it got under way. Several times his hands and feet slipped as he descended from his station.

The three were about half way down when Thorn turned his attention to them. "Here, you up there! One man can help Krause down. One of you get back aloft and keep the lookout manned."

Once on deck, Krause was laid out on a folded canvas, the wound was cleaned with water, and his companion dug the rest of the arrow out with his knife. He had lost considerable blood, and the wound was ugly. Thorn, though, appraised it with a comment about its slightness. Typically, he was impatient to return the injured man to full duty.

They had sailed for nearly two hours, covering approximately fifteen nautical miles, when a pleasant bay was sighted. On the shore stood a fair village. Lamazee called this the village of the Clallams, a group he had visited before. He looked over the rail without apparent apprehension, so the men judged these to be peaceful Indians. They recalled that as the Tatooche canoes approached Lamazee had cowered behind the gunwale.

Under Captain Thorn's direction, the TONQUIN was luffed into the wind, the sails were furled, and the anchor set. They had just completed these labors and were anchored in the bay when native canoes were seen approaching from the beach. Thorn again took the precaution of having some of the men armed, but unlike the previous encounters along this coast, these people arrived quietly and waited to trade.

A discourse between the redheaded intermediary and the leader in the nearest canoe brought the announcement, "They have few peltries to trade, some beaver but not many otter. They are poor people and wish a fair return for their furs."

"Ver-ry well, Mr. Ramsay," responded McKay. "Hae them fetch their peltries and we will give them a fair exchange."

"Just a moment," bellowed Thorn, "I won't have you giving away Mr. Astor's property."

"Nae one word has been said of giving, Captain, but the exchange should be fair, as these people hae requested." McKay seldom became angry. He was much more even tempered than McDougal, who had been in the forefront of conflict with Captain Thorn. But this interference in McKay's trading irked him.

Lamazee spoke a few words to the Clallam chief, and the Indians paddled back to the beach. In a short time they had returned with their meager stock. In the canoes were a few bundles of furs, principally beaver and fox. "Lamazee, is that all they have?" Thorn asked.

"Yes, they have been plagued with sickness and have become a poor people."

"Are there other villages along this strait?"

"Yes, they say there is another village called Elkwah about ten leagues beyond this village. I have not seen it, but the Yinnis and Tsewhitzen peoples are about fifteen leagues away."

Impatient as always, Thorn began giving orders to raise the anchor and set sails. He felt there would be little profit here so he intended to leave immediately. Both Lewis and McKay protested, but the orders were given. Dejectedly, the Indians looked on. It appeared that they would remain impoverished.

But fortune was with the Clallams. As much as Thorn fumed and stormed, the wind did not favor him. The TONQUIN was becalmed.

McKay was quick to sieze upon the the opportunity. "Quickly, Mr. Ramsay, hae them bring their peltries along side and we will do some trading."

The interpreter spoke, and with a shout, the Clallams were along side, climbing to the deck. Bartering was swift, furs for hatchets, knives, and trade beads. Thorn fumed even more about the trading than the lack of wind, making sarcastic remarks about the amounts offered for mere fox and beaver. For a while, though, he remained preoccupied with the ship lest the current carry the TONQUIN to a grounding depth.

A contest see-sawed back and forth as the current carried the ship toward shallower water then an off-shore breeze picked up for a moment and carried the vessel off and up the strait. The tidal flow out of the strait toward the open sea was increasing. In return, the gusts became stronger. Finally, the breeze became steady from the west, and the ship began to gather momentum.

By this time, most of the Clallams had exchanged their furs and were headed back to the village in their canoes. Only one more small bundle remained. "Get those filthy savages off the ship!" roared Thorn.

"Here," spoke Lewis quickly, holding a knife and some beads while pointing to the furs.

The two remaining Indians hesitated. Hurriedly, Lewis put the beads back on the deck and picked up a hatchet, now offering a knife and a hatchet for the bundle. The Indians nodded, took the objects from Lewis, and swung over the side toward the waiting canoes.

"Stop!" bellowed Thorn, "you are giving away valuable trade goods! Get those things back!"

McKay and Lewis stood looking at the captain as the Clallams pushed the dugout away from the side of the ship and started paddling. Thorn rushed to the rail, but the canoe was moving rapidly toward the beach as the TONQUIN gathered in the breeze.

"Mr. Lewis, I am going to log your deportment! Unless, of course, Mr. McKay shows the gumption to provide suitable discipline."

"'Tis nae a matter of discipline, Captain. This lad is my assistant, and I sanction his exchange."

Thorn turned red. "I shall log this incident, and describe the behavior of both of you. You may be traders, but any further mischief, and I will subject you two to the ship's discipline!"

They knew that this could only mean flogging, for Thorn used this form of punishment. Lamazee sensed this, too. He had unconsciously backed up against one of the masts. Now he was clutching tightly at his skin robe, as though someone might strip it from his back. He was confused. For a while he had identified with this captain who protected him, but now he could see himself as a trader lashed to the mast. He could feel the bite of the whip, and Captain Thorn became one with Captain Beasely.

The wind continued to be light that day, so it was well into the evening before a village, supposed to be the community of Elkwah, was spotted. It was small, and Lamazee assured the captain that the natives of this part of the strait were peaceful, but Thorn elected to secure with two anchors well out into the strait. He would take no chances of a surprise attack from natives who were unknown to him.

When both anchors were set to Thorn's satisfaction, a double watch was ordered for the night. Then he went below to make his threatened log entries. Lamazee remained on deck, withdrawn from both the crew members who were attending to assigned tasks and from the traders who were still inspecting and recording the acquired furs.

"What will Mr. Astor do when Captain Thorn gives him the log, sir?"

"Do nae worry, Jamie. If Captain Thorn gets back, there will be a few letters from his Pacific Fur Company employees, too."

"Sir, could we bother you for a bit?" It was one of the crew.

"Aye, what is it, laddie?"

"Would you have a look at Krause's leg, sir? It looks all red and is oozing something."

Following the sailor forward, he found Herman Krause lying on a bunk, moaning with pain. The light was dim under the flickering oil lamp, but the wound was obviously infected.

"Who was it that took the arrow from his leg?"

"I did," ventured one of the men.

"Are ye certain ye got it all out?"

"Yes, here it is," the man responded, holding up the barbed bone point and still-attached shaft. "I had to cut it out, but it's all here except the part of the shaft we took off up in the crow's nest."

"Aye, tis a wicked-looking thing with those barbs cut into the bone point. I can see why ye hae to cut it out.

"What knife did ye use?"

"This here one," the sailor stated, reaching into a sheath on his hip and producing a large, simple blade blackened by tar and rust and most recently stained with Krause's blood.

"Well, Herman may have gotten something in his leg from the arrow. It looks like blood poisoning. We hae better boil some water and put hot packs on his leg to see if we can draw the poison off."

Someone brought a kettle of hot water from the galley, and a few fairly clean rags. McKay applied hot compresses while a crewman held the lamp. Krause groaned and grimaced with each hot application but averred that the leg felt better after the care. His companions were instructed to apply hot packs at intervals during the night, and McKay would return in the morning.

One of the men walked with McKay to the companionway. "Sir, could we speak freely with you?" he asked as McKay was about to step out on deck.

"Aye, of course," McKay answered.

"Sir, we have had about enough of this captain. It is our vote that we relieve him of his command before he gets us all killed."

"You mean mutiny?"

"Sh-h, not so loud. Yes, sir. The way this Thorn goes around stirring up the Indians, he is going to have them lined up in their canoes just waiting their turn to shoot arrows into us. And they will, too, 'cause Thorn won't let us use the cannon. I, for one, don't want to die that way."

"What about the rest of the crew?"

"The men are all with us, and I don't think the mates would do much to help Captain Thorn."

"What is is you want wi' me?"

"Well, Mr. McKay, we figured you could take command and square it with Mr. Astor when we got back to New York, you being the senior partner on this cruise. I mean, you could do it legally. Just make Thorn give up his rank—with us backing you of course."

"I do nae like mutiny, but it may be the only way. I will hae to think on it a wee bit—but I will. I will let ye know in a day or two.

As McKay emerged on deck he noticed a shadowy form nearby. It moved slightly. Lamazee! He wondered how much the redhead had heard, and more importantly, whether he would go to Thorn with his information.

Fourteen

McKay went directly to the cabin he shared with Lewis and sat down. He thought for a moment, puffing on his pipe, then told Lewis of his conversation with the sailor. In conclusion he told of seeing Lamazee slipping from a place where the redhead could have overheard the talk.

Lewis was obviously distressed. "That could be very serious, sir. The scoundrel knows the crewmen have little respect for him, and he may suspect they feel he is in league with the savages. In a mutiny they would likely throw Lamazee over the side. His only chance would be to side with Captain Thorn. I'll wager he is in the captain's cabin right now, telling all."

"I do nae know, Jamie. This Ramsay fellow might not. Somehow, I can nae find it in my imagination to picture him facing the captain with tha' sort of story. He fears the captain and the authority the captain has. Furthermore, I am certain that Thorn would fly into a rage at the mention of mutiny. Aye, and Ramsay must be certain, too. I do nae think he is there."

Both men lay back on their bunks, sliding silently into their individual thoughts. Above deck the night passed peacefully aboard the *TONQUIN*. Below deck, while McKay and Lewis tossed with their thoughts of involvement in a mutiny, the slumbers of the off-watch seamen were disturbed by the moans of their feverish comrade. On deck Lamazee lay struggling with his own mental conflicts.

The morning dawned gray, with puffs of fog drifting past the tops of the masts and chilly drafts rippling the quiet waters of the strait. McKay and Lewis had arisen and gone out on deck but returned to their cabin for warmer attire.

Captain Thorn stood on deck studying the Indian village with his telescope. He was pleased, for trails of smoke among the trees suggested there were more lodges than had been visible near the shore. He counted fourteen canoes on the beach. This was a fairly large community, and trading should be profitable.

With the arrival of the first canoes, however, Captain Thorn scowled and became impatient. The furs were no better than those obtained the day before. McKay and Lewis could see his irritation and entered into brisk trading. The wind was not as calm as it had been when they had the unexpected opportunity to trade with the Clallams so the traders worked quickly, not taking the time to drive shrewd bargains with the Indians. At any moment, the unpredictable Thorn might order the ship under way.

The situation was not to Thorn's liking. Calling Lamazee aside, the captain ordered him to question the natives about other villages in the vicinity. Answers revealed that other tribes up the strait were more wealthy and might have better pelts to trade. The next community was only a few leagues away.

That was too much for Thorn. He ordered the ship under way. While the anchors were being weighed and the sails unfurled, McKay and Lewis continued trading. They purchased all the furs they could, and the Indians were obviously pleased with the exchange they received. Reluctantly, some villagers swung down the side to canoes, but others remained, striving to make better bargains. This angered Thorn, and he finally roared, "If those heathens don't get off this instant, I will throw them into the strait!"

Thorn's voice of authority and his manner needed no translation. Gathering up the remaining pelts and the goods that had been exchanged, the Indians headed for their canoes. Among the furs being carried back over the side were some excellent otter pelts. "Captain, I must protest," McKay interjected. "We are getting some good peltries, and many are being lost over the side through this halting of the trading."

"Protest and be damned! We are under way, and you can go over the side with the savages if you don't like it."

After the last of the natives had departed and Thorn had wandered forward to inspect the sails, Lewis turned to his superior. "Mr. McKay, I am ready to join with the crewmen. If we can't trade, there is no point to this voyage."

McKay didn't answer. He was looking at Lamazee who was standing silently nearby, watching.

The *TONQUIN* sailed easterly. By noon the lookout reported the smoke columns from another village. As the ship approached, Thorn brought out this telescope in order to study it more closely. This community was different. Situated far out on a narrow, sandy point, it was readily visible. It was unique, in that it was obviously fortified, and roofs were visible beyond the parapets.

"Captain Thorn, sir," the first mate interrupted, "shouldn't we veer off while we are out of cannon range? That looks like a fortified community, and it might be British. It isn't on the chart so it must be new. Do you suppose the reports of war being imminent might be true?"

"No, I have been looking it over well. There are no cannon, and it is not built in an English style."

"Well, sir, perhaps it is a colonial style."

"Carpenter, stop fretting like a housemistress. I see nothing but heathens moving about."

"Yes, sir."

"Make ready to drop anchor as soon as we are inshore to thirteen fathoms."

For nearly an hour the ship rode at anchor without a single Indian approaching her side. Canoes could be seen on the beach, but none of the villagers seemed interested in venturing forth. Impatient, as usual, Captain Thorn ordered the longboat lowered so Lamazee could be rowed ashore. It was Thorn's intention to invite the Indians aboard to trade.

The traders and crew watched the interpreter to gauge his reaction to Thorn's instructions. He did not seem as agitated as he had been when Thorn had dispatched him to the hostile beach, but he displayed no eagerness, either. It was difficult to tell what the risks might be. The third mate, Greeley, was the only one to express concern to the captain. In response Thorn flew into a rage, calling Greeley a coward in the face of a few sleeping savages. Summarily, the captain ordered the boat lowered and Greeley with four men to accompany Lamazee ashore.

At first the four men at the oars approached with trepidation. With their backs to the strange village, they could only watch the expressions of Ramsay and the man at the tiller. The interpreter was silent, giving them no encouragement. Mr. Greeley was still flushed after Thorn's dressing down, his jaw set. He might steer them right into the teeth of an enemy rather than return to confront Captain Thorn's displeasure.

Glancing quickly around, however, the rowers could see a group of women and children gathering on the shore. This was reassuring. Soon some men casually wandered over to join the gathering, and they appeared to be unarmed. The beach was peaceful as the longboat touched the shore. The surf was so mild that they were able to step ashore without wetting themselves.

Greeley and the seamen were amazed by the village they beheld. They had seen nothing like this among the communities of Indians along the wild coast. Nearest to them, almost at the beach line, were two rows of sharpened poles set in palisade manner, the highest wall being at least three times a man's height. Within the palisades was a large structure, well made, as though the natives had constructed it of huge sawn planks. It appeared to consist of many rooms and to be completely roofed. Into this Lamazee disappeared, but Greeley and the crewmen elected to wait outside. The interior was unlit and windowless, suggesting the many unpleasant possibilities that could be waiting inside.

They waited and wondered what mischief the redhead who had adopted heathen ways might be up to. The villagers they could see appeared to be paying little attention to the white men and were going about their tasks of placing clam meat on racks to dry, of carving a strange log structural piece, and of weaving fabric from strips of cedar bark.

Lamazee reappeared and announced that he was ready to be rowed back to the ship. Few men of the village had been apparent until this moment, and the sailors wondered, as they launched the boat, if they would be attacked. Rowing was more comfortable in this direction, for the oarsmen faced the Indians on the beach. Still, the natives paid little attention to them.

As the boat approached the TONQUIN, Captain Thorn appeared at the rail, shouting down to Lamazee, "Where are the villagers? When are they coming to trade?"

"They come later. Now they prepare a salmon feast."

"Don't the lazy dogs attend to any business?"

"They traded with a ship yesterday and have many knives, hatchets and beads. They ask for muskets and rifles. Many ships stop here; they are important people."

Cursing loudly, Thorn ordered the boat hoisted aboard, the anchor weighed, and sail made. He had had enough of this coast and was determined to quit it.

For the balance of the day the *TONQUIN* sailed on a westerly course. By nightfall the ship had cleared the strait and was traveling northwesterly along wild and unknown shores. McKay was again called upon to look in on the wounded sailor. Then stench was overwhelming as McKay entered the damp area of the forward section where Krause lay. He spoke to the man but received only mumbling in response. "What did you say, laddy?"

Again, the response was uninteligible, and Krause cried aloud as McKay pulled back the blanket to look at the wound. The leg around the wound was grossly swollen and dark blue in color. In the lower leg the man's skin was stretched so tightly that cracks appeared and bits of skin were peeling.

"What do you make of it, sir?" asked a crew member.

"It does nae look good. Hae ye continued to apply the hot packs as ye were instructed?"

"Yes, sir; well, the truth of it is, sir, that Captain Thorn has kept us pretty busy furling and unfurling sails and tending the anchors."

"Fetch me a sharp knife. I will try lancing the wound to see if some of the poison will drain off. Aye, and only if we had some leeches."

In time a knife was brought from the galley. McKay pulled the blanket back from the leg and placed his left hand near the wound in preparation to wield the knife with his right. Just his touch caused Krause to cry out in pain and draw his leg away. McKay also pulled back his hand, for the leg felt tight, as though it might burst.

"Aye, laddy, I ken your troubles, but we hae got to relieve that pressure in yer leg."

McKay motioned to Pennington who took hold of the injured man's shoulders while Porter cautiously held the leg. He cried out again as the trader pierced the wound. Some blood and discolored fluid drained but not the amount that had been expected. Nor did the swelling abate.

"Well, laddies, keep at the hot packs during the night, and we shall have another look in the morning."

The stench of the infected leg was such that McKay felt queasy. Instead of retiring to his cabin, he went up the companionway to the deck. As he stepped out into the fresh breeze, he caught a discourse between Captain Thorn and the first mate.

"The wind has turned smartly southwest, sir. Don't you think we should rig for a blow?"

"Not this time of year, mister. Don't you know this is the wrong season for southwest storms? By morning this will have blown itself out, and the clouds will have dissipated."

"Yes, sir, but should we take any precautions?"

"No! Tend to your duties, and check the watch."

"Aye, aye, sir." But as the officer looked up at the snapping canvas, a wind-whipped rain began to fall.

McKay finished his brief walk on deck without becoming thoroughly wetted by the rain and, feeling better, went below to retire. As he was falling asleep he gave no more thought to the discussion that he overheard.

The trader was not aware of how long he had been asleep when he sensed that the *TONQUIN* was pitching about more than normal. He came fully awake when the night was rent by a booming sound followed by ear-pounding flapping. McKay knew that a sail had ripped. Running feet on the deck above told him the crew had turned out to furl sail. Thorn had underestimated the storm front.

The traders' cabin was still quiet. Lewis had not awakened, and McKay was feeling thankful that he was not one of the crew and obliged to turn out in the wind and rain to furl and lash down canvas. He dozed off again though he braced himself in his narrow bunk so as not to fall out if the ship should roll wildly.

His sleep was fitful. The ship continued to pitch, and the more severe swells raised the bow of the ship to where it plunged with a jolt into the next wave.

On deck the rain drove through the rigging, now devoid of canvas except for storm sails. When the ship turned, heavy seas followed, and the largest of the following swells pounded against the stern. Often waves slopped over the taffrail and washed about the legs of the helmsman. After one large surge of water across the deck, the first mate ordered a line tied to the man at the wheel. This brought a scowl from Captain Thorn who still didn't want to admit that he had underestimated the potential of the weather.

In underestimating the force of the summer sea, Thorn had left the ship's only remaining boat hanging from its davits on the stern. In this position, across the stern, and crosswise to the swells, the little craft was frequently swept in its tackles against the ship. Little could be done about this in the heavy sea, for any man climbing over the taffrail would surely be caught by the waves and dashed to his death against the planking.

In time, with the faint light of dawn, the partially water-filled boat could be seen breaking apart with the longest of the plank seats pushed through the side. The gunwale toward the stern of the TON-QUIN was being flattened against the ship.

Dawn also found McKay in the foward compartment, seeing to the wounded man. Krause had spent a miserable night, for the motion of the ship had rolled him about, and each movement had been excruciatingly painful. As the trader approached, the man lay moaning in his bunk, beads of sweat on his forehead, his face flushed with fever.

"What do you make of it, sir?" asked a companion who was standing nearby.

"Well, we will hae to wait and see. If my fears are correct, though, the blood poisoning is well set in. The leg may hae to come off if we are to save Krause's life."

"Can you do that, sir?"

"I do nae know. I ne'er hae, though I once watched it back in the Highlands. 'Twas a surgeon that done it, though. It would be better to return to the post at the Columbia. Duncan McDougal, I ken, is better qualified than I, and he has some of the medicines in vials there that would help Krause get well."

"Then we should be coming about into the wind and sailing south. Will you talk to Captain Thorn about this?"

"Do ye nae think one of yer officers should do it?"

"They are afraid of Captain Thorn, sir. We tried last night, but not one of them would even come below to look at Herman."

"Ver-ry well, I will speak to the captain, but I do nae hold much hope of his complying with my request."

As McKay walked to Captain Thorn's quarters, the sailor, another, and then two more followed, until a group stood waiting a short distance away as the trader knocked on the door to Captain Thorn's quarters. The door opened, he disappeared inside, and the door closed. For a while the waiting crewmen could hear no sounds, but presently occasional raised voices could be heard beyond the confines of the cabin. In time the loud harranging of Thorn was unmistakable.

In the midst of one of the captain's tirades, the door opened and a red-faced Alexander McKay emerged.

"He wouldn't have any better chance with the butchering he would get from McDougal!" the captain shouted from behind the trader. "Besides, I won't sacrifice this expedition for the comfort of one scurvy sailor!" Thorn slammed the door without once looking out. Thus, he never saw the group of seamen awaiting his decision—and hearing his harsh words.

"Yer answer should be clear," commented the still-angry McKay as he stomped off in the direction of his quarters.

"Then we will have to take the ship," muttered one of the men.

This stopped the trader, who turned back to speak. "No, lads, let's not be in haste. Krause had a bad night, but his leg is draining. The sea is abating so he will be able to get some rest. Wait until this afternoon."

"If he isn't better and if Captain Thorn persists, will you join with us, Mr. McKay?"

"Aye, that I will." The trader turned again and walked through the companionway to the main deck. A shadowy figure was moving toward the starboard rail.

The balance of the morning passed normally. Sails were unfurled as the storm diminished, rigging was checked, and the main topgallant, which had split, was replaced. Little was heard, but wisps of conversation went on here and there any time two or more sailors came together, either aloft or on the deck. Thorn seemed unaware of the tension in the air, of the mutiny being plotted. In fact, he was pleased with the animated way in which the crew members were scurrying around.

Unknown to him, though, plans were being finalized. Pennington, who served as blacksmith, would break the lock of the arms locker while Reed acted as a lookout. Porter and an accomplice would fake an argument on deck to distract Thorn. They were certain that Carpenter, the first mate, would come to the scene of the disturbance as well, for he generally sought to be present at the side of the captain.

The second mate had been sick in quarters for the better part of the week and seemed no better today. One of the men would watch his cabin just in case, and Andrews would get the third mate, Greeley, to brag about his latest amorous conquests, a subject that the man never tired of discussing.

Some wanted to put Thorn and anyone loyal to him over the side in the damaged longboat. They would have little chance in a boat so weakened and with opened seams. It would be just as well, Pennington argued, to simply toss Captain Thorn and Lamazee over the side to swim for shore or drown. If they survived, they would be made slaves. Slavery, Pennington suggested, would be a fit punishment for someone as harsh and demanding as Thorn.

The ship's bell announced the end of the forenoon. McKay turned to see several of the crewmen looking in his direction. It was time to check on Krause's condition. The trader walked forward and started down the companionway, but hesitated at the sound of the captain's voice. "Are you going below to see to the sick?"

McKay wondered how much the captain knew. Had Lamazee spoken to him? The captain, however, turned his attention toward shore. They were approaching a rocky, wooded point with a reef consisting of many obstructions over which the surf constantly broke. Thorn was hoping to find the northern approach to Nootka Sound, but his sightings of the sun suggested that he was too far north.

"Mr. Lamazee, is that Nootka Sound?"

The interpretor shook his head. "Kyuquot."

Thorn immediately realized that it could not be Nootka, for the waterway stretched toward the northeast from the opening. The captain had revealed that he was unsure of his location, that he had navigated incorrectly.

"Is it a sound harbor?"

"Yes, Kyuquot has good harbor."

McKay went below but was quickly back, his jaw set and a determined expression on his face. The *TONQUIN* was passing through the reef, the lookout having found a fairly wide and deep entrance, but numerous rocky islets extended seaward from both north and south points. Beyond, on the port side, above an indentation that might serve as an anchorage, stood a village. Thorn directed the ship to that area.

"Is that a fit place to trade, Mr. Lamazee?"

The redhead nodded his head, with a trace of enthusiasm.

Thorn gave orders to make the anchor ready and was reducing sail. As one of the men rushed past McKay, he asked, "Have you looked in on Krause?"

"Aye," responded the trader. "He has taken a turn for the worse. The leg will have to come off, and soon. I will speak wi' the captain."

"And if he doesn't agree to return to the Columbia," asked the man, stopping, "are you with us?"

"Aye," responded McKay, nodding.

"Stop that gossiping and get to work, Folger!" bellowed Thorn. "What are you two up to?"

Seaman Folger went about his duties. McKay walked over to face the captain. "Captain Thorn, I have a ver-ry grave matter to discuss with you. I have looked at Mr. Krause's leg, and it is indeed much worsened. If we do nae obtain proper treatment, in fact, amputate the leg, the lad will surely die. I suggest we make great haste for Astoria."

McKay's last words were drowned out by a bellow from Thorn. It was first unintelligible, then the words boiled out, "I'll not turn back now! Stop your meddling—your damnable prying—into matters of this ship!" The balance of the deluge was a maniacal tirade. Flushing, McKay turned away and looked at the watching John Folger. The trader nodded his head.

"Forty fathoms," a man on the bow called.

"Summatlemulth," Lamazee muttered, then pointing to a native on shore, added, "he is a friend." The Indian appeared to be about to launch a canoe, but Lamazee eagerly added, "I go ashore, get trading started, much trading."

Word was being quickly passed among the crew. Thorn was still unaware that anything was amiss, but Greeley was talking quietly to Carpenter and looking about the deck. Lamazee glanced around furtively and looked a little pale as he moved quickly toward the davits of the longboat.

"Lower the boat," Thorn commanded. "You, Greeley, take Pennington, Sharpe, and those two," he continued, pointing to two men coming down from the rigging, "and put Mister Lamzee ashore. We will finally have some profitable trading going."

This move would rid the crew of one of the officers, but it would also deprive the mutineers of a key member, the blacksmith. Pennington was reluctant to go and stalled for a while feigning trouble with the fall block at the stern of the longboat. To his dismay, the interpreter approached and helped straighten the fall.

Captain Thorn came to the taffrail to supervise the lowering of the longboat. The craft had been badly damaged in the storm, and had not been adequately repaired, but with coninuous bailing it could make the short trip to shore. It was lowered to the water and began to leak as the four sailors manned the oars. Pennington glanced back up to the ship and noticed the captain had a pleased look on his face. He was probably expecting a wealth of furs, for the village appeared large and prosperous judging from the substantial construction of the houses and the number of carved poles in evidence.

The TONQUIN was close to the beach by the time it had reached a depth suitable for anchorage. Apparently, this part of the sound sloped rapidly. The trip to the beach was reasonably short for the longboat, and it was not long before Lamazee was ashore and mingling with the natives.

To the men in the boat, Lamazee's actions were disquieting. He was animated, it seemed, and his words were strange. They were accustomed to hearing "waa'com" or some similar word of friendship, but instead Lamazee seemed to be speaking of the ship, and the men in the boat, as "pushack."

"Mr. Greeley, sir," Sharpe asked, "what is this 'pushack' that Lamazee is talking about?"

"I don't know. I don't recall having heard it before."

Some natives launched canoes and headed to the TONQUIN with furs, but others were paddling their canoes rapidly in other directions. Words were being exchanged among the natives, words which alarmed the seamen for they prompted the Indians to glance at the men by the longboat.

"Mr. Greeley, I don't like the looks of those fellows, sir. And they're saying something else strange, this 'ill quaggeh.' What do you make of it?"

"I don't know, but you and Sharpe get aboard and bail the longboat out. I want it free of the beach—so we don't have to shove it clear."

"Yes, sir."

The boat was moved out and bailed, then bailed again. Still Ramsey lingered in the village. Some of the canoes that had left were returning with others following. So that was what they were up to. They were gathering the tribe. More canoes were seen in the distance, coming from what may have been a large island in the sound. Another village must have been located there.

"Come, Mr. Lamazee," Greeley called, "we best be going back to the ship. The traders will be needing your services."

"Not yet. Come, meet friends."

Greeley hesitated, but several women were with Lamazee, young women wearing cloaks that provided adequate glimpses of their charms. Greeley took a few steps closer.

"Come," repeated Lamazee, and one of the young women walked slowly toward Greeley. He went forward to meet her.

"Sir, don't you think you should stay with the boat?"

The men received only a wave in response. Greeley was arm-in-arm with the Indian women, heading for one of the houses. He would not return.

A large assemblage of canoes was around the *TONQUIN*. Many savages were aboard, more than it was prudent to admit onto the ship. However, many packets of furs were being taken onto the ship, and Captain Thorn was probably greedily encouraging more.

Lamazee appeared briefly, long enough for Pennington to call to him. "Mr. Lamazee, come fetch Mr. Greeley and let's go."

There was no answer. Lamazee disappeared into a house. A few men appeared on the beach, looking toward the crewmen.

"I don't like the looks of those fellows. The older one has a spear."

"Yes, and the others have war clubs. I'm sure that they didn't a while ago. Where are Greeley and Lamazee?"

"Lamazee! Mr. Lamazee!"

"Let's get in the boat and move off a ways. We can watch for Mr. Greeley and Lamazee and pick them up when they come out."

Slowly, casually, the men joined the other two in the boat and allowed the craft to drift away from shore. Pretending to be getting ready to move back to the beach, instead they set the oars and moved off. They continued until they were out of range of spears and a difficult shot for arrows. Neither Lamazee nor Greeley were anywhere to be seen. The beach was nearly deserted.

Across the placid waters a commotion was heard aboard the ship. Thorn's voice could be clearly heard. He was in fine form and thoroughly dressing down some hapless person. Then a native came tumbling overboard, followed by another. Thorn had previously threatened to throw visitors who displeased him into the sea, and now he was carrying out his threats. For a moment it seemed that the canoes would fill and disperse, but the Indians were climbing back onto the ship.

Pennington turned and looked back toward the shore. The interpreter was standing near the entrance of one of the largest of the wooden lodges. Some women were carrying something out and tossing it onto the beach, something that looked like a bloodied body. "Look! That's a body, ain't it?"

"Yes, it looks for all the world like poor Greeley."

Another commotion. This was more general, and there were many voices, not just Thorn's. Had the mutiny started? The men started to row toward the ship. Shots rang out. No, it wasn't the mutiny. Lewis fell bleeding over the side to land in a canoe and be stabbed to death by Indian women waiting below.

"Those damned savages! Now we know what Lamazee was up to. The words we didn't know were inciting the Indians to make war!"

The men rowed on. Others were seen falling or being thrown from the ship and then stabbed to death in the water. The crew was vastly outnumbered by hundreds of savages. Then the fighting on deck ceased. Only Indians were seen moving about the deck. For a while men had been in the rigging, but even these were gone, brought down by showers of arrows.

The men in the boat stopped rowing. "We can't get aboard now; we had better row around the ship and try to make it out to sea."

Shots, muffled shots, showed that fighting was still going on below deck.

"There's that scoundrel, Lamazee, there on the beach by that canoe. He was in league with them!"

True, he was there, speaking with a group of Indian women.

"They must be getting ready to loot the ship. Lamazee will be a wealthy man with a whole ship full of trade goods, even firearms."

"Yes, but we better bail this boat out and get rowing hard, we've a long way to Astoria. All is lost here."

So it seemed. The ship was swarming with natives, resplendent in beads and bright bits of cloth. Busy as they were with their looting, they paid no attention as the longboat passed, heading for the Pacific.

Then it was all gone. As the men in the boat looked back from their oars, the ship flew apart in a cloud of smoke, masts, rigging, deck, and Indians. Someone, perhaps Thorn, had touched off the powder—the gunpowder the captain had been saving. The impact of the blast reached their horrified ears and bits of debris began to rain from the sky. The tan arm of a recently victorious warrior dropped near the boat, sinking in a dark swirl.

For a moment all was quiet except for the splashes of still-falling objects, then the sounds of the blast echoed repeatedly from picturesque islands and distant ridges along the sound.

The men rowed on. In the distance they could hear the groans of the dying. Screams came from those who discovered the loss of father, son, daughter, brother. The smoke drifted away, leaving a bitter residue upon water which was again quiet. Then the attention of those in the remaining canoes turned to the longboat striving to escape.

The leaky boat was no match for the canoes of angry savages. Long before Pennington, Sharpe, and the other sailors were able to reach the open sea, the savages were upon them, tearing at them viciously with knives and spears.

On the beach, one remaining canoe was being launched. Not rushing out to help injured survivors struggling to hold onto bits of planking or a fallen mast, not joining in the last bitter fight, it held only one shadowy form. Silently, it moved along the south shore, blending into the dark forms cast upon the waters by trees and rocks. It slipped away toward the open sea.

Months of surreptitious, solitary travel brought the red-head back to the land of the Killamuks. Henceforth, he avoided the traders at the fort, and the Pacific Fur Company learned of the *TONQUIN*'s massacre only through stories brought by Indians of the north who came to fish in the Columbia.

Fifteen

The dream had faded from McTavish's mind, but the world of consciousness had not yet returned.

There was a shot. John was instantly awake, aware that the shot had been fired nearby. Feeling around in the darkness of the hut, he found his rifle, checked the priming, and pulled back the heavy hammer until, by the click, he was certain it was cocked. He had not fully risen from his sleeping position. Carefully, he studied each feature of the shelter softly visible in the dim light. No one was there, not even McDougal. Had he wandered outside and been attacked? Were the Nehalems waiting in ambush? McTavish got up quickly, moved to the small ports that faced the sea, and peered out. Beyond, the western sky was lit with the reflected pinks and yellows of the sunrise. Tinted breakers placidly tumbled on an empty beach.

He turned back to the opening which faced the village. It was not quiet in that direction. Wailing and moaning sounds, low at times, then increasing in pitch and volume, drifted with the breeze. McTavish listened. Were the sounds coming from the village or from the sandspit? As the awesome sounds filled the air, he realized that they were coming from both directions.

Cautiously and slowly—as silently as possible—he moved to the entrance. He could hear more clearly. They were women's voices. This was not an attack, for the sounds were those of mourners, not warriors, and the sandspit had become the resting place of another victim of the pox.

McTavish came out slowly, looking first on the roof, then toward the village for possible ambush. Rifle ready, he walked from the hut staying clear of walls or bushes that might conceal an enemy. The area around the hut was empty.

In the damp sand a single pair of footprints led from the hut. Nearby was a set of circling prints left by a dog. John followed the man's tracks, puzzled that they did not move toward the village but around it, toward the mountain. As he walked through the dunes, he glanced back toward the village. Some Indians had been aroused and now appeared with bows and arrows. They conversed among themselves briefly then also moved in the direction of the mountain. John sensed that they were not hostile but were investigating as he was. Taking separate paths, John McTavish and the Nehalems moved on.

He was topping a dune when he saw McDougal. His partner was in a small hollow surrounded by scrub pines. Duncan was bent over, working on something, and was partially hidden by a small tree.

"M'Dougal, wha' are ye doin'?"

"Fetching some proper meat so they don't eat Roamer. I have slain a venison."

"Aye, that ye hae."

The thought of fresh, cooked meat was invigorating. It was apparently stimulating to the Indians, too, for they quickly gathered around. Their talk was more animated than the traders had previously observed, and for the first time since their arrival at the Nehalem village, they saw the glimmer of rising spirits. Perhaps Yakala was right; a good meal might return the will to survive.

When Yakala arrived, Duncan rose and spoke. "We have taken as much meat as we need for our meal. The rest of this venison is for your people. May it help them to regain their strength."

"Klo nass," Yakala responded, "it may help their spirits. Our people have been sick and weak too long to have the will to hunt. Thank you."

Turning, Yakala gave instructions to the other Indians who had gathered. A young man, Kwalim, took charge of skinning and cutting up the animal, and his companions eagerly joined in.

The two white men returned to the shelter where they had spent the night. On the side away from the beach and wind, which had increased, they built a fire of bleached driftwood. As they prepared their meal, they could also observe the activities in the village.

"Look, Duncan, they hae dug a pit and are building a large fire in it."

In a short time a fire raged the length of the rectangular hole the natives had dug in the sand. Women were tossing large stones into the coals of the fire. Out on the tide flat, now exposed by receding waters, other women poked about with sticks. Occasionally they reached down into the sandy mud, withdrawing clams and placing them in baskets. Some gathered seaweed into bundles.

McTavish's vision traveled from the activity on the tide flat, on across the flowing waters of the bay, and came to rest on something unusual. The tide was low, and two rows of posts disturbed the gentle flow of water where it neared the far side. He stood up for a better look. There, like a blackened skeleton displaying two rows of immense ribs, stood the wreck of a ship. It cast sinister shadows upon the rippling water.

"Aye, M'Dougal, tha' must be the ship, or what the Indians hae left of it."

McDougal arose from tending the strips of venison over the small fire and climbed onto the sandy hillock closer to the bay. Roamer took that opportunity to snatch one of the strips of venison, dropped it when it burned his mouth, then lifted it gently from the sand and ran off. McDougal frowned as he glanced back but said nothing to the dog. He know that were it not for Roamer he would probably be carrion.

"Yes, it certainly looks like it. I am surprised at the size, though. It is much smaller than the *TONQUIN* or the *RACCOON*. In fact, I wouldn't make the hull to be more than sixty feet. It probably wasn't over seventy in overall length before the bow and stern were burned away."

"Tis a wee one and would have been terribly cramped on a long voyage." McTavish stood beside McDougal for a while, silently looking out upon the dead ship. Then he added softly, "Interesting, is it nae, tha' e'en in death, resting in these waters, it looks dark and sinister?'

For a while Duncan McDougal also looked silently at the dark form with blackened ribs reaching claw-like from the water. The void between the ribs was filled with rubble and long strands of sea grasses that had taken root there. "Yes, in a way. I am not sure, though—any burned vessel is going to look black. I suppose you are referring to that vivid dream you had about this ship."

"Aye, Duncan, but tha' dream was different. It was so intense and so real. I hae had only one other quite like it, and tha' was last night."

Before McDougal could respond, he noticed that Roamer was returning. If they were to have any venison themselves, they would have to hasten back to their campfire.

The two turned their meat and resumed their observations of the activities in the village. Glowing coals and equally hot rocks remained in the fire pit. Upon this bed was placed a layer of seaweed that steamed and smoked, hissing loudly. Then chunks of venison, clams, and even a few crabs which had been raked from the shallow tidepools were placed on the steaming seaweed. A final layer of seaweed was placed over the food, and all was covered with sod. Only a few ribbons of rising steam suggested the nature of the mound.

The Nehalems had created a great bakeoven. While their food was steaming and simmering, the Indians were bustling about, conversing excitedly. Compared to the atmosphere of the village when the traders arrived, the mood was festive. People prepared utensils and baskets, or stood talking in small groups, watching the cooking mound. A few children frolicked playfully.

When the mound was broken into, and the food distributed, the community again settled into silence. Everyone appeared too busy feasting to talk. Only the starving dogs rushed about, quarreling noisily over scraps. Roamer had joined readily into the fray and was more than holding his own against the less-muscular local canines. Soon, even the appetites of the dogs were satisfied, and serenity reigned. Indians sat before the lodges, others lay stretched out in the sun. Most were probably uncomfortable from overeating.

At this point Yakala came to continue his visiting. "Ah," he commented, "that was good venison." He belched loudly as though to emphasize his statement, then sat down slowly.

McTavish turned in the direction of the bay and the blackened skeleton now disappearing beneath the waters of the incoming tide. "Those blackened ribs in the bay, are those of the *RAVEN*—the ship Lamazee arrived in?"

Yakala started, tensed, and appeared to be about to rise to a standing position. "You know what the bear-people called their ship. You were friends of those people?"

"Oo-h," McTavish flushed, stammered a moment, then added, "No, I was guessing at the name. Did ye nae say it was as dark as a raven?" John did not wish to reveal the dream of the preceding night.

Yakala was unconvinced. He turned to McDougal. "You, from the other bear-people, but you—you have hair that has some of the fire in it. You are the smallpox chief, are you not, the one with the sickness kept in the bottle? Will you make war on us? Our people have suffered much already."

"No," McDougal shook his auburn-haired head. "I am called the smallpox chief, and I do have the bottle at the fort, but I am not a friend of the men of the dark ship.

"I don't plan on making war on your people. We have come, as we have stated, to trade for your furs."

Yakala was still uncertain, his gaze going first to McDougal, then to McTavish. Finally, rising and turning to face the waters of the bay, he said, "Yes, that is all that is left of the great sail canoe. It was closer to the village but fled while it was burning. As the flames leapt high there was a great rattle of the chain that held it in place. Then the chain slipped into the bay, and the great canoe turned up the river with the tide and to the shallows with the wind. It rested where you see it.

"Lamazee was dismayed, for he wanted it to sink out of sight. But, the water where it rests is not great enough."

"Then Lamazee became one of your tribe?"

"Yes, after a time. But before I tell you all there is to know of Lamazee, will you promise not to open the bottle and send more evil spirits to make war on us?"

"Yes," McDougal answered, "so long as your people trade and dwell in peace with us, we will not make war on you."

"Would you do one more thing? Would you, oh smallpox chief, cast a spell to make our people well?"

McDougal hesitated. He turned toward McTavish who was looking toward the village. His facial expression was intense.

"What do you think, John?"

"Well-ll, M'Dougal, the disease may have run its course. I hae nae heard any wailing since early this morning. It might nae hurt to try."

"Yes, perhaps you're right." McDougal looked at the village where the children were again playing. "Very well, Yakala. The venison I gave to your people was the first medicine to make them well. If you will tell us all there is about Lamazee, and later, when we return, show us where the men of the RAVEN placed the chest of yellow metal, I will cast a spell for you."

Yakala winced at McDougal's final condition. For a time he studied the auburn-haired Scotsman, then answered. "Yes, I will tell you, and I will show you where the chest is if you will tell no one else and will take it directly away—far away from our village, that no one may know or see it."

understand neither his strange words nor his actions.

"Finally, toward morning, tired from her efforts as a wife and cold from the dampness after the storm, she turned away to cry. Lemolo curled up to go to sleep. And then was when Lamazee took her—in very low form. How could one be tamanawash and take his mate in the manner of the lowly dogs of the village?"

McTavish nodded. He understood, for he realized that it was probably the only form of sex the redhead had known. It was closest to what he had suffered as a wretched cabin boy.

"Loatle was elated when he heard the story and used it to break the spell of Lamazee. Soon some of the villagers again listened to the medicine man and scorned the red-haired man. Kwetl, one of the young women of the village, laughed and set out to taunt Lamazee in her own way.

"She was a bold one and plotted an adventure with the strange man who had come with the bear-people. She was curious and wanted to experience him for herself. So, she watched and waited. At times Lamazee took his thunder club and hunted by himself. Kwetl followed him stealthily one day, and when the hunter was far from Nehalem in search of game, she revealed herself to him.

"Without her clothes she taunted him. At first he seemed to ignore her, but she continued. She followed Lamazee, placed her body next to his, then laughed and ran away. Returning, she placed his hands on her chest, and when he clung to her, she pulled him to the ground. They rolled about together in the forest, and Lamazee learned to make love like a man.

"Kwetl returned to the village and told the other young women of her adventure. She laughed as she described Lamazee's clumsiness in making love. Loatle had taunted the redhead, calling him dog-man; now the young women laughed at him as a bad lover.

"Lemolo heard the stories and was angry. But, she was his wife, and benefited by Lamazee's new knowledge. She also tried to maintain the favor of the Nehalem for her husband. She reminded all who would listen that they enjoyed the wealth of the ship because of Lamazee, and his thunder club had made their war parties strong." Yakala paused, allowing his audience to absorb the strange tale. He knew that if his village were not in such extreme sorrow he would not have been so free with his words.

"Through the winter," Yakala continued, "the wealth of Nehalem diminished. Slaves died or ran away, and it took too many beads and hatchets to buy more. The men lost most of their pieces of metal in their gambling and asked Lamazee for more. He had none. Shilthlo asked for more of the magic powder for his thunder club. Lamazee could not supply it. The thunder clubs and their power were lost. Loatle ranted about the weakness of Lamazee's spells.

"Spring came, but the salmon were few. Loatle was quick to blame this on the spells of Lamazee. It was true that the red one contributed little to the catching of the salmon. The great fish were not content to be caught by the redheaded one and repeatedly dodged his spear. Even when he had the fish, they wriggled out of his hands. He also lacked the skills of hunting even the children of Nahalem possess. When the fire-and-thunder sticks were useless, we found that Lamazee could not use the bow and arrows. They would not go where he commanded. Loatle laughed at him and said that Lamazee was weak."

"Then it was Loatle, the medicine man, who ran Lamazee from your tribe?" asked McDougal.

"No, not yet. I will come to that. There is much more to tell before that part of the story.

"As the people of Nehalem became poorer, more turned against Lamazee. Lamazee thought of other ways to regain wealth, but no wealth was gathered. A small group of bear-people came past the great mountains to see the land of the Clatsops, and we planned to take their wealth and thunder clubs. One of our villagers tried, but the bear-people had been warned by the Clatsops. We waited for them to come to our lands, but they did not, and one winter they returned to their homes.

"Time passed as Loatle and Lamazee matched their spells, and both of them remained as tamanawash. However, Lemolo had to be content with the clams, crabs, berries, and roots she could gather and the occasional fish and game Lamazee could overcome.

"Then a man returned from the land of the Clatsops, telling of a great sail canoe. Lamazee said it would contain much wealth. He said he would cast spells so that the Nehalems could capture that wealth and would go to look upon the sail canoe.

"Loatle warned that the red-head's spells were weak and that bringing the sail canoe to the Nehalem could bring many demons upon us.

He feared the bear-people would raise the spirits of the slain men and urged us to send Lamazee away. Lamazee boasted that he could work his spells elsewhere and then return with wealth. He would not have to share the wealth if the villagers of Nehalem would not help him.

"So it was that Lamazee went to the great sail canoe—and it was great, for its trees were taller and the canoe much larger than our largest lodges. He went into the sail canoe, and it went away with him to the land where the goose goes in summer.

"The moon had waned and returned several times before Lamazee appeared before our lodges again. He was tired and had not eaten for many days. There was no wealth, only a small canoe which he had stolen and a new knife. The sail canoe was no longer, he said, and he could not go back to it for wealth. Lamazee told us the spell had worked, but the bear-people had used the magic powder to destroy the sail canoe and all that was in it."

"Aye, tha' would hae been the *TONQUIN*?"

"What did you say? Were you speaking the name of the sail canoe?"

"Aye, was it called the *TONQUIN*?"

"Yes, I think that is what Lamazee said the bear-people called their great canoe."

"Go on, lad."

"Many of the people were disturbed. Loatle raved that the proof was there, that Lamazee's spells had failed. Then the illness came again. Oclallah's family was stricken, and several in his lodge died. Wauclahan became ill, and though he lived, two of his slave wives and four of their children died. Illness also came to Ishta and Tuckwah, but none of these were friends of Lamazee. The redheaded one was quick to point out that his friends in the lodges of Seanow, Washecal, and Wy Kee Kill had not been struck down by the spirits. If Loatle was so powerful he should be able to protect those who favored him.

"The people began to listen to Lamazee again, and, since those in the lodges of Oclallah and Wauclahan died, many thought Loatle's medicine was evil and planned to kill him. Lamazee must have known his spell would not last, however, and distracted our people with plans to sieze your lodges. He took some of our warriors and journeyed to the land of the Clatsops and the great river, there to view your fort and lodges. The Clatsops, though, warned our people of the power of the smallpox chief, and our warriors lost heart. Then some of your men surprised them in the forest, and they fled."

"Aye, tha' was the time we caught a glimpse of that red-haired scoundrel when we were out hunting. Now we knew why he rushed away wi'out talking wi' us."

"While Lamazee was away, those in Ishta's and Tuckwah's lodges recovered, and Loatle regained his place in the village. The sickness had been bad enough, though, that the people of Nehalem had become poor of canoes from using them to bury their dead.

"Other sail canoes came to the land of the Clatsops, but Lamazee would not go alone to work his spells upon them. Even he was losing faith in his spells, and no one in the village would go with him. All feared the bear-people and the smallpox curse, for we were feeling the ravages of illness and wanted no more spirits of the slain to deal with. We stayed away from the other canoes."

"I suppose, John," McDougal interjected, "those were the American ships, *PEDLER* and *BEAVER*."

"Aye, though it could hae been the *RACCOON* and *ISAAC TODD*. But, mon, we are interrupting wha' the lad is telling us."

"I do not know how you call those sail canoes, but Lamazee feared to go near them. He thought they might have learned about his spells and would kill him in most savage ways."

"Is that when he left?"

"No, I come to that now. When he returned from casting his spells so that the people where the cold winds blow would attack the great canoe you call *TONQUIN*, Loatle taunted him. When he returned again after the warriors were frightened from the fort, Loatle and his apprentice, Cheumas, stood in the trail as Lamazee approached, chanting and shaking their rattles. They said they were breaking his spells on Nehalem.

"Many of us ignored Loatle and Cheumas, for we knew the rivalry. That fall the salmon run was good. Even Lamazee caught many fish. All were able to dry many fish for the winter and to prepare much food from the berries of the hills. With the food from the sea added, it looked like it would be a good winter. Loatle's claims were ignored. Lemolo bore a baby so the stories of Lamazee not being a manlike lover grew old. Loatle no longer raved. He only grumbled and waited.

"Then as the winter rains diminished and the flowers of this spring came to the meadow, the illness came back. As we were preparing for the new salmon feast, Lawsuk screamed that her son was sick with the pox. Loatle shook his rattles, chanted, and claimed to have seen a vision of the spirits of the bear-people killed by Lamazee's spell in the cold country. He said they had followed the redhaired one to Nehalem and that they had joined with the spirits from the dark ship to make war on us. Lamazee tried to cast a spell, but the child died, and more became ill. Loatle, too, tried to appease the spirits, but still the sickness came. The only way to stop the plague, he whispered, was to kill Lamazee.

"As the salmon appeared we could not harvest them, for we were unclean and some of our dead were still above the ground. As soon as we could wrap one in lisquis tipsoe mats and placed the body in a canoe for burying, another would die.

"Some of the men were slain by those at the fort, but we were too weak to avenge them."

"Ah, so that is why your warriors didn't come. But," added McDougal, "the men that were killed at the fort were being punished for murdering the woodcutter. Their punishment was just. The men at the fort were not making war on you."

Yakala sat silently for a while, looking at McDougal. Duncan began to wonder if his threat during the early days of the post to release a bottle of smallpox spirits against the Indians held any sway now. They were already beset with smallpox.

"The ways of all the Killamuks has been to take blood debt. But fear not, for our warriors have lost their will to fight. Look at those empty lodges," Yakala went on, pointing to silent structures nearby. "Those were the homes of Ishta, Tuckwa, Tuckoquise, and their families. Only a few children live! They have banded together in the lodge of Swiliuse, for his hut was nearly empty.

"Look on, and see that all of the women have cut their hair short for mourning. You must have heard the wailing this morning as the sun rose.

"Loatle chanted, raved, and shook his rattles, but he was unable to save our children. Even his apprentice, Cheumas, was stricken by the bear-people spirits. When he died, the people turned on Loatle and set upon him with sticks. We thought that might appease the spirits, but it didn't. The next morning Loatle was dead."

Yakala shook his head sadly. He was fighting to hide his emotion, but the depth of his depression was obvious. His silence was respected by the two white men, and all three sat quietly for a while. It was McDougal who asked, "What about Lamazee and his friends?"

Then Yakala raised an arm and pointed toward even more smoke-less, voiceless lodges. More moments passed before he found his voice. Then, slowly and haltingly, he said, "For a time Lamazee's friends and his family were charmed. The spirits had waited, but they came to Lamazee in time.

"Those silent lodges belonged to Seanow and Wy-Kee-Kill. Few of their families are left, and they have gone to dwell in other homes. Both had large families, for Lamazee had been generous with his friends, and they had slave wives to increase their children. Those lodges had three families each, with happy children who laughed as they chased the little crabs along the beach and raced to see who would go in the canoe while their father caught fish. The wives were good workers, gathering many roots, berries, and clams, making many blankets of skins, and bearing many children. Now all are gone.

"Lamazee yet remained. He claimed he knew an Echanie, a supreme God not known to the people of Nehalem. The villagers waited.

"Neither Echanie nor Talapus would hear Lamazee's pleas. He had cast too many evil spells, and all of the spirits of the slain bear-people were coming for him. Lamazee's friends were dying. Lemolo became ill, and then the baby. Both died. He had lost Tamanawash and could save nothing from the spirits he had offended."

Now Yakala was animated. His face, earlier drawn with despair, was twisted with hate. He stood up, raised a clenched fist and almost shouted, "Lamazee promised us great wealth; he brought misery, guilt, and death, terrible death to our children, our wives, all of us.

"But his spell was broken. We knew we had to kill Lamazee to appease the spirits of the dead. There," Yakala continued, suddenly pointing to the blackened pit were a lodge had stood, "was where the evil one dwelled. We took up our spears, clubs, and bows and gathered at his hut. We called for him to come out, but he did not. He stayed inside, wailing like a child. So we set fire to the cedar planks.

"As the fire roared brightly, and smoke from the house filled the air around us, Lamazee slipped through a wall. Most of the men were waiting at the entrances, spears and clubs in hand. The smoke stung our eyes. Lamazee, alas, was already running from the Nehalem before he was discovered. His legs are longer than ours, and he was soon beyond the reach of our spears.

"Our bows and arrows were the only hope. But, each time we stopped to shoot our arrows he moved farther from us, and it was difficult to hit him as he ran among the dunes and small trees. He ran toward Neahkanie. Perhaps the fire spirit will punish him. That is what may have been intended."

Three men, one primitive and two from a new, encroaching civilization, sat silently upon the sand, their backs to the rumbling of the sea. They contemplated the scene below. Smoke rose from some of the lodges, marking families that would remain a little longer. Children scampered through cedar huts, ducking into openings and emerging from the far ends of the dwellings. Women moved about with baskets of firewood or busied themselves with other chores. Village dogs frisked about the lodges, occasionally growling noisily. All three men sitting on the dunes wondered how long it would be before this scene vanished.

What lay ahead for little Nehalem children like Esahtin Neslasht? Would future generations in this valley even know family names like Teewint, Skallah, or Sweliuse? Lamazee was no longer present to exert his evil influence, but the effect was there, and vengeance seemed ready to take another people.

"I have told you all there is. The yellow metal is yours also. You need only follow the river—so." Yakala pointed, then drew a crude map in the sand. "When you come to this small stream, look for a mound above the fork. It is on the hillside at the height of the river-bank trees.

"Now, will you make some magic to help my people?"

"Yes," McDougal replied. "Your people have eaten of the meat I gave you and are better. I tell you to also harvest the salmon and send your women, with baskets, up the trail my companion and I arrived on. They are to gather the many berries that await and prepare them for the winter."

"Yes, but what of some magic signs? My people need a sign." Yakala turned toward the village, rose and beckoned. Some of the villagers noticed and came, curious, to where the men talked.

"Let me go with my friend into the hut for a moment to prepare myself."

Yakala nodded.

The traders withdrew. "What am I going to do, John?"

"Aye, I hae been giving tha' some thought, Duncan. I also noticed our cooking fire still hae some embers. I kicked it as we came away to be sure. Take some gunpowder in your hands and drop it on the embers. When the smoke rises, raise you arms and start shouting."

"What? What will I shout?"

"What'er comes to your mind, mon. Make it a prayer, if ye will. In fact, a prayer might be in good order to get us safely out of here."

Duncan held out his hands, and John poured powder from his powder horn into each one. The two returned to Yakala and the few waiting villagers.

Without speaking, Duncan walked toward the group, stopping over the campfire site. He glanced down briefly, turned to hold Yakala's gaze, and dropped a handful. Nothing happened.

McDougal stepped to one side, hoping for better aim with the other handful of powder. He hadn't seen the embers that John had mentioned but dropped the other load anyway. Still nothing happened. Unconsciously, he rubbed his hands together and looked down at them. No, the gunpowder didn't show. Well, he would have to think of something or do something, but he couldn't seem to work himself into a shout.

He kicked sand slightly by the fire. Whoom! Duncan was engulfed in fire and smoke. He jumped slightly—he hoped not noticeably—as he held his breath in the acrid smoke.

The breeze moved the cloud enough that Duncan could stop squinting and look out. Yakala and the villagers had retreated wide-eyed. McDougal thrust his arms up sharply, took a breath, and shouted, "Oh, Lord! Talapus and Echanie! Look after these murdered victims, and make these people well! This I implore of you!"

Wheezing, he turned and walked through the drifting cloud of smoke and rejoined his companion.

"Mon, that was a marvel to see. I thought ye had blown yerself up. Ye looked and sounded great."

Duncan coughed slightly. He turned to see what the Nehalem people were doing. They were talking excitedly among themselves, occasionally looking up onto the sand dune where John and Duncan still stood. Yakala was nodding.

Sixteen

Duncan noticed the position of the sun and realized it was mid-day. In the sun's tranquilizing beams, those women who had not taken their baskets and set out to collect berries were weaving mats of cattails from the riverbank. The men of the village sat about talking or watching two youths who were hewing a large cedar log into the shape of a canoe.

Three men sat upon the dunes, their bodies warmed by the sun. They relaxed and quietly watched the peaceful scene in the village below. No one spoke until Duncan McDougal rose and turned to his fellow Scotsman. "M'Tavish," he spoke softly, but his companion was deep in thought. "John M'Tavish," he spoke again.

McTavish looked up. "Wha' is it, mon?"

"We had best be on our way, John. The men back at Fort George will be worrying about us. Aside from that, we should be on our way in case my spell doesn't work. And, if it does," a hint of sarcasm entered McDougal's voice, "it might be so strong that the warriors recover their desire to fight and to extract that blood debt."

Yakala overheard the conversation, and rose to speak to the traders. "Do not fear. We would not slay the smallpox chief who has called away the spirits of the bear-people. Besides, ah-ee, there are so few of us remaining. The men of Nehalem are no longer to be feared."

"Aye," McTavish replied, "but M'Dougal is right. We should be crossing yon mountains while the day is bright. The lads at the fort will be needing us."

"How did you travel to our village?"

"We came by land," McDougal answered. "We walked down the beach to the far side of that cape then followed the stream inland past the village of the Nehaynehum. M'Tavish climbed a great hill to find the route into your valley. From there he could see your land and out into the ocean."

"Yes, yes," Yakala responded, nodding. "That was Swallalacha, where dwells the maker of thunder and lightning. She, Hahness, once lived where the goose goes in winter but came to this land to become the bride of the fire spirit. It is a good sign that you were guided here by such a great spirit."

McDougal waited a moment, reflecting that such an omen might help to protect them from attack by Nehalems or others of the Killamuk tribes. Then he went on, "From there we crossed a ridge and found the trail that led us here."

Yakala nodded. "And it was along that trail that you saw the berries you offer our people as further medicine against the spirits." He seemed pleased, for in his primitive thinking a pattern was developing. Talapus must have sent the smallpox chief and his companion to Nehalem.

"Will you return the same way?"

"It is the only trail we know. If there is a shorter way back to the land of the Clatsops, we would be obliged if you would direct us to it."

"The path by which Hahness sent you is not the way we usually travel. It is the way we go when there is a great storm upon the sea and strong winds blow. It is a longer way to the land of the Clatsops, but it is safer when the powerful wind-forces are upon us.

"There is a shorter way, across the slope of Neahkanie that faces the sea. It is narrow, though, and where it crosses the slope, there," Yakala pointed to an almost sheer face of Neahkanie mountain where it dropped into the Pacific, "the path is difficult to follow. We use it on days like this when the gods of the sea are quiet. It can save you many hours of travel."

"That sounds good, doesn't it, John?"

"Aye. Will you show us how to reach it?"

"No, I am becoming too old and my legs are still weak from the spells of the spirits, too shaky for so steep a trail. But Kwalim will guide you through the dangerous part of slope. I will fetch him."

With that promise Yakala left the traders on the dunes and walked back to the village. He spoke to some of the women then, following the direction of one who pointed, disappeared into one of the lodges.

"M'Dougal, is yer ankle ready for this trip? It sounds as though the path may be a wee bit stoney and steep."

"I think so. It seems less painful and swollen today, and I have been walking on it. Before we start out, though, I will bind it."

Duncan sat down and wound strips of cloth around his ankle. When he was done both men arranged their packs. They were ready to travel when Yakala returned.

Kwalim was with Yakala. The two Indians were talking as they approached the traders, but John and Duncan could not make out enough familiar words to know what was being said. Still lacking trust in the Killamuks, this conversation concerned the traders.

"This is Kwalim," Yakala said. "He does not understand any of the language of the bear-people, but I have told him to guide you over the rocky part of the trail to the place where the path goes into the forest. From there the route is easy to follow."

McTavish greeted the newcomer, extending his hand. "How do you do, Kwalim." The boy stood staring back, saying nothing and making no effort to accept the outstretched hand. McTavish was unable to read anything in the boy's expressionless face.

"He does not understand what you say or your custom of taking hands," explained Yakala. "He has never been to your Fort George and did not know the bear-people of the dark ship. They had been slain before Kwalim was born.

"He knows the trail, and will guide you safely. Kwalim has been to the land of the Clatsops several times."

McTavish faced Yakala and extended his hand again. The older Nehalem man grasped it.

"Thank ye for yer hospitality, Yakala. We ken how difficult this time of illness and mourning must be. We grieve wi' ye for the lost Nehalem people and pray to our God as well tha' the spells of Lamazee are broken. We hope tha' the remaining members of the Nehalem tribe will live in peace and prosperity."

Yakala's facial muscles were slack, his jaw drooping in sadness. The aging Indian gazed into the distance as he responded, "The spirits of the dead will live with us. Those who remain thank you and the small-pox chief for coming to us in peace. His gifts—the venison and the berries—and his spells have begun to make us well. Already we have taken heart.

"I fear, however, that the evils of Lamazee's spells have already been cast. The many tormented souls of those he lured into death are waiting all around us. They will fall upon us again, for we have failed to avenge them by destroying Lamazee."

Neither McDougal nor McTavish spoke. Despite vast differences in culture, they understood the primitive man's feelings and knew that there was nothing they could say to ease his sorrow.

"Go," Yakala continued, grasping McDougal's hand also, "and may Talapus drive all evil spirits and savage beasts from your path."

McTavish and McDougal shouldered their packs and picked up their rifles. Yakala made a gesture to Kwalim who started off and glanced back to see if his charges were following. McTavish called to Roamer, and they were on their way.

Yakala watched for a while, standing atop the dunes, then slowly returned to the Nehalem village.

They traveled in single file, Kwalim in the lead, then John McTavish, Duncan McDougal, and the dog sniffing along behind. The Indian boy took them across the dunes and along the beach toward the huge, looming cliffs of the cape standing before them. They had walked for an hour at a brisk pace when large stones began to replace the sandy beach. More rocks, black from the moisture of the waves and rounded from rolling in countless breakers, appeared. They seemed to outnumber the grains of sand. They picked out sandy strips between rows of stone, but finally the sand ended. McDougal was falling farther and farther behind, struggling to protect his ankle from the terrain. Roamer had left the slippery rocks and was somewhere in the bushes above the beach.

McTavish was torn between concern for McDougal and his desire to keep their guide in sight. He didn't want Duncan so far behind that he would be without assistance, but he didn't want to become separated from Kwalim. In spite of his short legs, the boy was setting a brisk pace. Warriors with endurance like Kwalim's, John thought, must have given Lamazee a thorough chase.

Anxiety for his companion finally became great enough that John stopped. "Duncan," he called out, "are ye all right?"

"Yes, but the footing on these smooth rocks is very unsteady. I have slipped twice and fear that I might have made my ankle worse. Where is our guide?"

"I do nae know where Kwalim is. He seems to have left us, and it appears to be a solid wall of rock ahead. Ye better have yer rifle ready in case he has led us into a trap."

However, Kwalim had not left. They soon saw him standing just beyond the rocky beach, looking down from a thicket of stunted pines.

"Wha' do ye think, M'Dougal?"

"I don't know. Perhaps that is the trail."

"M'Dougal, let us go above the beach here and move through the pines toward him. Tha' way we won't be any more in the open than Kwalim is."

"Yes, that would be wiser."

The traders turned and climbed above the beach. Following the edge of the shore, they made their way toward the spot where their guide had last been seen. Walking in the soft sand, hampered by stunted trees and dead branches was no easier than struggling over the slippery rocks. Cautiously, they proceeded until they came upon Kwalim.

There he stood, silently waiting for his two charges to catch up. When they arrived, he turned and started out again, following a distinct path that wound through the dunes and small trees. Several paths branched out, but Kwalim strode confidently ahead. The side paths intrigued the dog, who made sorties first in one direction, then the other.

As they reached the slope of the mountainside only one path continued, its edges bounded by a thick matting of brambles that reached higher than the travelers' heads.

"Well, M'Dougal, the lad seems to know what he is aboot."

"Yes, we seem to be able to trust him. I guess he is taking us out of danger."

"Aye, and I notice Roamer is nae alarmed."

Duncan didn't respond to John's expression of confidence in the dog. Instead, he changed the subject. "From the beach this looked like a steep meadow, but it certainly isn't. I wish we could see where we are going."

It would be hours before McDougal would get his wish. In the meantime, the brambles were so thick that not even Roamer was able to leave the path. At one place a small rabbit ran across the trail, but the dog could not make his way into the rabbit burrow. Struggling to get their breath after a particularly long and steep stretch, they broke out onto a rocky face where only a few stunted bushes grew. Stopping, they looked back toward the land of Nehalem.

"My God," McDougal exclaimed. Below them, to the south, lay a panorama unlike any he had ever seen before. From the base of the cliff upon which they were standing stretched an immense sandy peninsula, thickly wooded on the landward side and glistening with sand dunes and beach at the seaward edge. Its western border stretched off in a nearly straight line toward the distant horizon. Where the ocean met this peninsula, rows of white-capped breakers swept restlessly onto the beach. To the east shone the quiet waters of the Nehalem Bay. Above the background of the bay, from a location hidden by tall evergreen trees, curving ribbons of blue smoke rose from the village. Beyond, the sharp, forested peaks of a rugged but fertile mountain range were visible.

For a while the two white men stood in awe.

Then McDougal and McTavish turned back to the pathway. Ahead was more open, rocky terrain. Between the barren spots, patches of scrubgrass and spindly bushes grew, and occasional upthrust jets of basalt interrupted the steep slope.

"Aye, M'Dougal, 'tis a stony path. Will yer ankle take it?"

"I think so, John. We will just have to move carefully. Besides, we can't turn back now."

"Aye, mon, I would nae like to lose this day's travel, but wha' is the path like ahead?"

The trail became steeper. Often the footing was on solid rock that slanted toward the sea, but at times they crossed loose rock that rattled and slipped as they traversed rockslides. Any bit of soil, any vegetation with holding roots was welcome. For as they struggled along the meager path the ocean roared beneath them. Looking down, the men could see the tremendous spouting spray as foaming breakers assaulted the very cliff they were crossing.

Kwalim, however, was not looking down. Neither was Roamer. The boy's attention seemed to be upon the mountain peaks above them. Roamer looked upward and sniffed the wind. The hair on the back of his neck was raised, and he emitted an occasional low growl. Both occasionally stopped and stared upward, watching and listening.

"What is it, Kwalim?" McDougal asked.

There was no reply.

"He does nae ken yer question, Duncan."

"I know, but both he and the dog have been watching for something up the hillside. This would not be a very good place to fight either savages or beasts. We best move on."

"Aye." The trail continued across the steep rock face. McDougal and McTavish listened and watched as they moved along. Although Kwalim stopped several times, the traders were unable to identify any particular sound.

They were again in broken rock when McDougal's ankle gave way, and he fell. He had stepped upon a loose boulder the size of a man's chest, and it had rolled, causing his foot to twist. Duncan grasped for a handhold, but slid down the rocky face. John rushed forward, but he was too far away. Duncan and the boulder were sliding down the slope.

At last, McDougal caught hold of a bush. It tore loose, its roots shallow upon solid rock. He grabbed another. It held. His momentum arrested, Duncan rose to his knees for better traction. Below him, the rock continued to bound and plunge down the slope until it disappeared over the precipice to fall into the sea.

"Duncan, how is yer ankle? Here, mon, let me give you a hand."

McDougal accepted the outstretched hand and pulled himself up to the trail before responding. "I don't think it is hurt beyond what it was, but let's rest a bit before going on."

Kwalim also sat down a little farther along the trail. He waited patiently, but continued to study the hill above them.

"Do ye hear anything up there, Duncan?"

"No, not clearly, though a while ago, just before I fell, I thought that I might have heard a wolf in the distance."

"Well, we have nae been bothered by them around the fort, though I hae been told they are native to this country. 'Tis strange we hae nae seen any before this."

McDougal flexed his foot and pronounced it well enough to continue. "As soon as we come to some decent shrubs, though, I will cut another walking staff," he added.

Beyond, the slope abated and the footing became more secure. Soil clung to the rocky crevices, and patches of brambles and scrawny, distorted evergreens finally gave way to solid masses of the same thorny bushes they had passed through at the base of the rocky cliff. As the path led over a crest, the Nehalem land was no longer visible. McTavish stopped for a moment and looked back, a touch of anguish in his heart.

The little group moved ahead through what would have been a

pleasant mountain valley if it were meadow instead of brush. Between them and the bluffs leading to the sea, tall trees grew in scattered thickets; ahead of them, and above, was forest. It was here that they stopped to listen again. Perhaps because the roar of the breakers was farther below them, all three were able to hear the sounds from high on Neahkanie Mountain. At first they felt more than heard the wailing. Then the eerie sound was certain. Roamer sniffed the air and growled again.

The travelers pushed on, but stopped again shortly. Above them were distant outcroppings of rock. Between the rock bluffs were thickets of sheltering trees, forested creases in the mountainside that continued toward the rugged peaks above. From one of those sheltering groves came the sound. It was animallike, but somehow human. McTavish had heard it before—in his dream of the first night of their voyage. It was the hysterical crying of a frightened child.

"What a weird sound," McDougal remarked. "I have never heard a catamount wailing quite that way before."

McTavish was shaking his head. Kwalim was silent, but his hand was upon the handle of the knife in his fur sash, and he gripped it so tightly his knuckles were white.

McDougal was confused. "It isn't a catamount? What is it, John?"

"Lamazee."

Seventeen

"What did you say?" questioned McDougal, but Kwalim was nodding sternly. "Lamazee," the boy repeated. For the first time on the trip he showed some emotion. His face was grim, twisted with hate, as he stood looking up the mountain. Perhaps he was thinking of following the sound, trying to avenge his people, but the crying seemed to be moving quickly up through the timber. It was fading even as they stood there.

A short ways beyond, the trail followed a gentle slope and the brush gave way to young evergreen trees. To the west, and slightly south, a point of land sloped away, then gently curved upward, ending in a promontory capped with stately trees. Through the trees ahead, a stream could be seen leading to a steepsided cove. Kwalim stopped, waved his hand forward along the trail, then turned, and, without a word, departed in the direction from which they had come.

McDougal poked around in the brush until he found a small alder tree from which to make a walking stick. While he shaped it, the two adventurers sat and rested. For a while they glanced back along the trail. Kwalim's disappearance had been so sudden that they found themselves expecting him to reappear at any moment.

"Do you think there is any danger of getting the boy's knife in the back?" McDougal asked, looking up briefly from his whittling.

"No, if anyone has anything to fear from the lad, it is Lamazee. If he has nae returned to his people, he is probably hunting through the thickets on the mountain."

McDougal grunted. He sighted along his walking stick, apparently satisfied.

"Well, M'Dougal, are ye ready to press on? How is yer leg?"

"Yes, I think I am ready. My leg is well enough to travel some more though it *is* somewhat swollen." Duncan was favoring his leg as they continued.

The trail led them out of sight of the sea and into a shaded canyon. For several miles they followed the small stream as it wandered, murmuring through the valley and out onto a barren hillside that faced the ocean. This time, however, the footing was not as treacherous, nor the slope as steep. Nightfall found them tired, but upon the crest of a mountain from which they could see a fair beach. They were not yet back to the land of the Clatsops, but they were sure that it was not far away. Another day of travel should bring them back to Fort George.

They decided to make camp in a small but dense grove a short distance above the trail. "Shall we build a fire, John?"

"It would be a wee bit of comfort, and we can place it between those two logs where it can nae be seen from the trail if we keep it small. Aye, let's light one, Duncan."

They were right. Night brought damp winds from the sea. The warmth of the fire was comforting. Roamer stretched out beside it and was soon fast asleep. The two men sat in silence, warming their hands.

It was McDougal who interrupted the quiet. "This will certainly give Thompson something to write in his journal."

"No, Duncan, I do nae think we should tell them very much."

"Why, M'Tavish?"

"Think, mon. If they learn aboot the treasure, the men of the post will be clambering over each other to come dig it up. The Nehalems will ne'er hae any peace. I hae a bad feeling aboot visiting this land again—at least for a time."

"Yes, and we can return to get the gold later. We would be rich."

"I do nae know, M'Dougal. The treasure has a spell upon it. Let it rest a while."

"What will we tell them at the post?"

"Simply that the Nehalems have not come to trade because of a plague."

Silence settled over the weary travelers. In the distance, absorbed by the forest, sounds drifted through the darkness. The sounds were those of hysterical sobbing, of a boy who was abused and whipped upon the mast, of a man who had lost his world and lost himself to his fear.

Epilogue

In the spring of 1973, a scuba diving buddy, Irv Jones, and I were exploring part of Oregon's Nehalem Bay when we came upon an unusual mass of rock. Although the rocks lay in a pattern like the ballast of a ship, they were not quarried rocks like those I had seen in the remains of *WAR HAWK*, *ALETA*, *WELCOME*, *AMERICA*, or other wrecks I had visited. No confirming evidence of a shipwreck, like timbers, ribs, or metal fittings were present, so Irv and I passed the rockpile by.

Publications like The Smithsonian Institution's "History Under the Sea" alerted us to the fact that English merchantmen of the 16th through 18th centuries commonly used "Coarse gravel" as ballast. A discussion with Ralph Mason, then a geologist with the Oregon Department of Geology, confirmed that what we had seen could not have been a natural deposit for the described rocks were not native to the area.

Irv and I returned to study the site, but could not find it. Two years later, a channel change uncovered the rocks again, and samples were taken. The October 1975 *Ore Bin*, a publication of the Department of Geology and Mineral Industries, provides the results. "Geology establishes that the Manzanita wreck is not a local vessel, for the ballast found low in the pile (and thus mostly likely original ballast, since to remove all ballast is to invited capsizing) includes quantities of gneiss and quartzite, both uncommon in the port areas of the western United States but common rocks of Europe. Other rocks unfamiliar to our Pacific shores but possibly from Mexico, such as dacite, suggest a stop along the way." According to Ralph Mason, the stones were beach rocks (as opposed to the quarried rock normally used in 19th century and later vessels). They had also clearly lain in ballast, for the softer rocks had grooves worn in them while the harder rocks had matching polished spots.

Pre-19th-century vessels were also apt to contain no metal below the water line. Instead, planking was attached with treenails (large wooden pegs). This partially explained the absence of small metal fittings. Not yet explained was the absence of large metalic items like capstan, rigging, and anchor.

In addition to the geological samples, physical characteristics of the pattern were measured. Its 30-by-13 feet, blunt-ended configuration matched the armed schooners that made their appearance around the time of the American War of Independence. These were about 70 feet in overall length, 50 at the keel line with 30 suitable for ballasting. Ballast was not usually included in the pointed bow and tapered portion leading to the rudder. The depth of the ballast, averaging two feet, also suggests this size of ship.

A lateral trench, dug through the ballast pattern while searching for identifiable pieces of wood, revealed a scattering of bricks in the lower layers. These were marked, some red bricks bearing "Ravens, WBI&Co." and a number of broken buff examples with "—ottle" (all with the last part of the marking). Basil Saffer, Curator of the General Shale Museum of Ancient Brick in Johnson City, Tennessee, stated the bricks were made with techniques that were in use "not much before 1800." For nearly a year, despite contacts with brick collectors and archaeologists we were unable to identify the markings.

Finally, responding to an article in *Brick & Clay Record*, the international trade publication of the brick industry, J. T. Kailofer, DIP-CERM, LICERM, wrote from England. By the markings, later confirmed by chemical matching, he identified the bricks as having come from the village of Walbottle near Newcastle-upon-Tyne, England.

Not stopping there, Mr. Kailofer made extensive contacts, discovering that there had been a group of "merchant venturers" operating illegally from Newcastle at the time that the ship appears to have been operating. These commercial pirates were known to have been in the Pacific Northwest since they brought back cargoes which included sea otter pelts. The sea otter trade began after Captain Cook noted their abundance in 1792 and continued through the balance of the 1790s. No records of their ships and crews are available as these entrepreneurs, who traded without the consent of the King, kept none that would reveal where they went and what they did.

History records that a red-haired caucasian with "Jack Ramsay" tatooed on one arm was living among the Indians of the Nehalem area when Lewis and Clark made their expedition to the Northwest in 1805-1806. Ramsay, Mr. Kailofer reported, is a common name in the

Newcastle area.

Ramsay told explorers and traders that he was the son of a man who jumped ship and took an Indian woman as his bride. This we know, from the study of genetics, could not have been true, for Jack Ramsay had the recessive traits of bright red hair, fair skin, and blue eyes. Nehalem myths tell of the red-haired "god" that rose from the sea, and there are tales of a ship that came and went many times and which left buried treasure on one occasion.

The Nehalems were silent on the subject of massacre. However, other Indians passing through told fur traders of seeing the Nehalems massacre the crew of a ship. At this point the evidence is circumstantial, but the ballast pattern is approximately across the channel from the site of the Nehalem village. Nehalem tales also tell of the use of bits of iron and copper in their gambling games. Archaeologists have found metal objects, thought to be pieces of ship's hardware, in excavations of Tillamook Indian villages. Is that where the metal from the upper portion of the ship went? The ship lies in water so shallow that at extremely low tide one can stand up on the ballast pile in water only up to the thigh. So the Indians could have stripped it. Or perhaps they burned the ship for its metal content and to hide their murder.

Assuming that the ship met its fate in the mid or late 1790s, one consideration is what age Jack Ramsay would have been at the time of its loss. Unfortunately, Lewis and Clark, who first reported Ramsay's presence, recorded no estimate of his age in the log of their explorations. We do have later references from the journals of the North West Fur Company that would have placed the redhead at the age of a cabin boy, perhaps ten or twelve, about the time the ship was entering the Nehalem River.

Some accounts refer to Lamazee rather then Ramsay (Emund Fanning spells it Lamayzie), the way Jack pronounced his name. We can only surmise that a rough outlaw crew would have abused a boy with a speech impediment. Such a boy might have sided with the Indians —or even incited an attack as a means of revenge.

Records do establish that when the Astor party arrived at what is presently Astoria, Oregon, in 1811 and set up a trading post, the ship that brought them, the *TONQUIN*, continued north. It was never heard from again; only an interpreter who had been taken aboard returned to tell of the massacre (to Captain Sheffield of the brig *HER-*

SILLA in 1823, twelve years after the loss). That interpreter was "Lamazee." What role did he play in the *TONQUIN* tragedy?

There is more circumstantial evidence. There are fables of the "Treasure of Neahkanie Mountain," thought to have been buried north of the Nehalem estuary just beyond Manzanita, Oregon. This cache of gold objects is believed to have been stolen from Spanish missions along the Mexican coast. Perhaps this explains why the wreck ballast contains dacite, not common to the Northwest coast or Europe, but common to the coastal areas of Mexico.

Death has sealed the lips of the participants in these events. Not even whispered stories, handed down from generation to generation, can be studied, for there are no more Nehalem Indians. Of the signers of the 1851 treaty, many left no heirs to receive their portion of the settlement. By 1871, when the first post office was in operation in the area, there were only 28 Nehalems left. By the mid-1900s, all had vanished. Lamazee, it is said, lived out the rest of his life along the coast of what is now the State of Washington. He passed away without revealing the truth of his origin in the wilderness of the Pacific Northwest. Any other truths which he might have revealed will never be known.

We have only the wreck and the limited historical records: the log of the Lewis and Clark expedition, the records of the Astor party, the journals of the North West Fur Company which acquired the Astor post in 1812, and such early observations and writings as Ross Cox's "Adventures on the Columbia River."

Photograph by Dean Bisping

JAMES SEELEY WHITE is a native of the Pacific Northwest. A naturalist and expert diver, Mr. White is the author of *Seashells of the Pacific Northwest* (1976) and *Diving for Northwest Relics* (1979) as well as many articles for *Diver* and *Treasure* magazines.

Library of Congress Cataloging in Publication Data

White, James Seeley.
   The spells of Lamazee.

   1. Lamazee—Fiction. 2. Tonquin (Ship)—Fiction. 3. Nehalem Indians—
Fiction. 4. Indians of North America—Northwest, Pacific—Fiction. 5. North-
west, Pacific—History—Fiction. I. Title.
PS3573.H4728S6 1982   813'.54   82-14578
ISBN 0-932576-12-5 (pbk.)